BOUND BY TROUBLE

BEACH BOUND BOOKS AND BEANS MYSTERIES

BOOK 4

CHRISTY BARRITT

River Heights

CHAPTER 1

So far, the grand opening of Beach Bound Books and Beans had been a smashing success.

Thanks to the help of everyone on the island, Talitha Robinson had been able to open her bookstore and coffeehouse months ahead of her original plan.

Locals had told her Lantern Beach needed an establishment like hers—especially during the winter months when there wasn't much else to do on the island. Tourists were gone. Beach weather was hibernating. Most stores were operating on limited hours.

Standing on the edge of the crowd, Tali held her Westie, Sugar, and watched all her favorite people mingling amidst the comforting scents of coffee, cinnamon, and vanilla. Outside, pumpkins, hay bales, and friendly skeletons decorated storefronts as the fall season swept over the area.

Life didn't get much better than this.

"I'm really proud of you, Tali," a deep, rich voice said beside her.

Mac MacArthur appeared at her side looking as handsome as ever in his black cargo pants and blue Henley shirt—one that showed his still-defined muscles. The former police chief and current mayor had thick white hair, beautiful blue eyes, and reminded Tali slightly of Mark Harmon of *NCIS* fame.

Tali grinned up at her friend. "Thank you, Mac. I can't believe this is really happening. It's everything I ever dreamed it would be."

"You deserve all the good things, Tali."

Her cheeks warmed at the affection behind his words.

The two of them really needed to talk. And they would.

Tomorrow at breakfast.

They couldn't put off their conversation any longer.

Tali's gaze wandered over everyone at her shop. Members of her book club had joined her as well as friends from church and numerous contractors who'd helped her get this place ready. Even Police

Chief Cassidy Chambers had come.

Her gaze stopped at a fortysomething man she'd never seen before as he lingered in the corner. He had a pointy nose, a thin layer of sweat covered his brow, and his business casual clothes seemed out of place in the beach town. He held a cup of coffee like he was trying to blend in, but something about the balding man seemed awkward.

He'd glanced at Tali several times since he'd arrived, but he hadn't spoken to her—or to anyone, for that matter.

Tali hadn't opened up this event to everyone on the island—she couldn't accommodate them all. So who was this stranger?

Even more, why did he seem familiar? It didn't make sense.

"What is it?" Mac leaned closer and followed her gaze.

She nodded toward the man. "I'm just wondering who he is."

"Maybe he's a visitor who heard about your shop opening and decided to come out for it." Mac shrugged as if it weren't a big deal.

Tali nodded and tried to loosen her shoulders. "You're probably right."

Before she could think about it any longer, the

door opened, and another flood of guests joined them.

The two gorgeous women bringing up the rear of the group caught her eye. One was in her late fifties, with bobbed dark hair, a thin frame, and puckered features. The other was thirty and also thin with dark hair but had a more relaxed, friendly demeanor.

Tali hadn't seen those faces in a long time.

"Deanna? Maisie?" Tali couldn't believe it.

Her sister-in-law and niece were here.

They hadn't told her they were coming to Lantern Beach.

Tali excused herself from Mac and wove through the crowd until she reached them. She observed them both a moment before pulling Maisie into a hug. Sugar wriggled in Tali's arms, sneaking a few licks to Maisie's chin.

"I can't believe you two are here all the way from Georgia!" Tali squealed.

Or that they'd come out for her opening. Tali and her niece Maisie were close. But her sister-in-law had always been cold. Deanna wasn't exactly the supportive type—not just of Tali, but of essentially anyone in her life.

Deanna gave Tali a stiff, obligatory hug before glancing around the shop. "This is quite the place you have set up here."

Tali beamed as she looked at her little shop with the exposed brick and the deep-blue walls. Bookshelves accentuated the space, and a live edge wood counter was positioned in the corner where coffee and treats were served. Conversation areas had been set up in any other available space.

She wanted this to be a gathering place, somewhere people could come together to enjoy coffee, talk about books, and share their lives with one another.

Community. That was the main word that came to mind.

All her hard work had brought her vision to life, and it was like a dream come true.

"It certainly is . . . *crowded*." Deanna said the words with disdain.

Tali ignored her negativity and practically beamed instead. "I know. Isn't it great? This island has been so wonderful to me since I've arrived."

That was if she didn't include the dead bodies and crimes she'd encountered since she'd moved here. But this wasn't the time or place to bring *those things* up.

Before she could say anything else, her phone buzzed. She'd gotten a text:

I'm looking for Stephen King's *Misery*. Do you

have a copy in your shop?

As a matter of fact, she did. But she wouldn't respond right now. She'd wait until later when there wasn't so much going on.

As she scanned the crowd again, she looked for the man she'd been observing earlier.

But he was . . . gone.

How had he left? If he'd gone out the front door, Tali would have certainly seen him since she was standing right beside it. The shop had a back entrance that required walking through the office and storage space. Tali hadn't kept the door between the spaces locked because that was also how the bathroom was accessed.

But why would he leave that way?

A sense of foreboding stretched between her shoulders.

"Is everything okay?" Maisie studied Tali with concern. "You're frowning."

Maisie was observant—just like her uncle, Tali's husband, had been.

"I'm not sure." Tali pulled her gaze away from the crowd. "It's just that—"

Before she could finish her sentence, a loud bang split the air.

Gunfire.

A single shot.

The blast sounded as if it had come from right outside her store.

————

As soon as Mac heard the gunshot, he searched the crowd for Tali.

She still stood near the front door.

Looking shaken but okay.

His shoulders softened, but just barely.

"Stay where you are!" Cassidy shouted to everyone in the room.

Before anyone asked any questions, Cassidy and Mac raced outside and glanced down the boardwalk. A cold late October wind brushed over them as they stood there.

But they saw nothing.

"The gunfire must have come from the back of the building." Urgency stretched through Cassidy's voice.

As they both headed in that direction, Cassidy put her phone to her ear and called for backup.

They rounded the corner and spotted a man slouched against the building.

It was the stranger Tali had asked Mac about earlier.

As Cassidy checked his pulse, Mac scanned him.

He didn't see a weapon in the man's hands.

That must mean that someone had done this to him.

But the darkness around Mac acted as an accomplice to the culprit, concealing his whereabouts.

"Are you okay on your own here?" Mac glanced at Cassidy.

Cassidy nodded and stripped off her sweater to press into the man's wound. "I'm fine. I'll try to slow his loss of blood until paramedics get here."

"I'm going to see if I can find this guy."

She gave him a knowing look. "Be careful."

Mac had served as police chief on this island for thirty years until Chief Bozeman took over for a few years and then Cassidy came along. Mac liked to think that he'd taught Cassidy everything she knew. But Cassidy had come well equipped with ample intelligence to figure things out herself. Still, he acted as backup whenever she needed him.

Mac considered which way he should go.

If this gunman had run, he hadn't gone to the front of the building. Mac would have seen him. So that left the beach . . .

He ran to the edge of the boardwalk, toward the dunes lining the area. Using the light on his phone, he illuminated the sand, searching for footprints.

They'd be hard to see tonight, especially since a hefty breeze shifted the sand, smoothing any indentations left there. He looked around, but nothing notable stood out to him.

With no time to waste, Mac surveyed the entire area. The man could have run behind the line of buildings and darted into one of the alleyways.

Mac turned and took off in that direction.

CHAPTER 2

"What's going on here?" Deanna looked horrified, almost as if she'd walked into a crime-laden, rinky-dink town well below her social status.

"I don't know." Tali gripped Maisie's arm. "But we need to stay calm. Maybe it was just a firecracker. Either way, Police Chief Chambers and Mac are looking into this."

Tali knew that sound hadn't been a firecracker. But her words seemed to make her niece feel better for a moment.

Almost as soon as she'd said the words, sirens wailed in the distance.

More help was on the way. That brought her a small measure of relief.

But she was still shaking.

Tali had lived here for four months, and this was the first time she'd ever heard gunfire in the area.

She swallowed hard, feeling the urge to somehow protect the people who'd come to her shop for her grand opening. The nurturing side of her felt responsible for every single person in her bookstore. They'd come to support her. She couldn't let any of them be hurt.

"Excuse me a minute," she muttered to Maisie.

From across the room, Tali's gaze met Axel Hendrix's, a former Navy SEAL and Mac's good friend. He had ushered people away from the front windows and stood between them and the door.

She cut through the crowd and headed toward him, knowing he would help her.

"What can I do for you, Tali?" he asked.

"Can you lock the back door, just to be safe?" To be truthful, Tali was too frightened to head to the secluded area herself.

He nodded and disappeared into the office area. As he did that, Tali quickly double-checked the lock on the front door.

It was secure.

But would locking everyone in keep them safe?

Or was she trapping everyone inside with a killer?

As Tali second-guessed herself, she scanned the crowd.

The cheerful, carefree atmosphere that had been present only moments ago had disappeared as fast as hot coffee being flash frozen.

Tali glanced around one more time, trying to determine if anyone had left.

But the only person she noticed missing was the out-of-place stranger.

Tali held Sugar closer, using the dog as a comfort blanket.

With all that had happened here, Beach Bound Books and Beans might as well change its name to Prison Bound Crime and Corruption.

———

Mac took off in the direction he thought their gunman had retreated.

Backup should be here soon. He already heard the sirens heading this way.

But time was of the essence right now. He couldn't let the shooter get away.

He ran past the surf shop, the toy store, and a gift shop. The back of these buildings faced the ocean, and the alleys between the shops had trash cans and AC units that were mostly tucked behind screens so no one would see them. That left a lot of nooks and crannies to hide in.

In the distance, he spotted the pier. Spotted the giant Ferris wheel that had already shut down for the season.

But where was the man?

As he reached another set of buildings, he paused and peered around the corner.

Nothing.

He let out a long breath, everything surprisingly quiet around him. He should hear footsteps or a car door slamming or wheels spinning against the pavement.

The quietness had him on edge.

Where had this guy gone?

Poor Tali. All she'd wanted was for the grand opening of her new bookstore and coffeehouse to be a smashing success. She'd used those exact words several times.

And now this.

It seemed like trouble followed her wherever she went.

A bad feeling brewed in his gut, and Mac slowed his steps, knowing he had to be careful.

As he passed a dumpster, something darted out in front of him.

He braced himself and reached for his gun.

But instead of a killer, a black cat appeared.

Mac muttered to himself before letting out a breath.

The feline looked up at Mac with annoyed green eyes before rubbing itself against the trash container.

"Just you out here, huh?" Mac quickly rubbed the cat's head. "Don't scare me like that again. Understand?"

The cat let out an aloof *meow* in response, and Mac continued on his search.

Who was that man who'd been shot? Mac didn't recognize him, so he was probably a tourist. The strange thing was, Tali had limited the invitations to a select group of island residents.

His curiosity grew.

He continued behind the building, keeping his eyes open for anyone or anything that appeared out of place. The smell of homemade fudge from a nearby store mingled with the salty scent of the ocean. Sweet and salty—that could often describe island life.

This guy hadn't simply disappeared into thin air.

He'd gone *somewhere*.

As Mac glanced down an alley, something metallic creaked above him.

Just as he looked at the fire escape zigzagging there, something crashed into his head.

Then everything went black.

CHAPTER 3

Tali glanced around her shop again. Despite the music playing in the background, tension grew in the air. Everyone murmured to themselves and glanced toward the windows as if expecting the worst.

Deanna and Maisie stood near the coffee bar—Deanna appearing annoyed, and Maisie frightened. Tali had handed Sugar to Maisie and asked her niece to keep an eye on him.

Sugar was the best security blanket ever.

Tali had also sent her friend Serena over to talk to them as a distraction. The outgoing girl didn't know a stranger.

Tali glanced around again.

Where were Mac and Cassidy?

Shouldn't they be back inside by now?

She'd heard the sirens and seen the flashing lights outside her window. She knew backup had arrived.

Cassidy had instructed her to stay inside along with everyone else.

Tali tried to obey the rules—most of the time, at least.

But right now, all she wanted to do more than anything was to step out there and see what was happening.

That's when she realized there *could* be another way for her to find out information.

She grabbed her phone and pulled up security camera footage from outside.

She hit Live and a video of Cassidy standing over a man who lay unmoving behind the bookstore filled her screen. Two paramedics examined him while a couple of officers wandered nearby.

Someone *had* been shot.

It wasn't until that moment Tali realized she'd been holding out hope that the gunman had missed his target.

Tali wanted to raise the volume so she could hear the conversation, but that felt too intrusive. Plus, anyone else around her might hear what was happening also.

"Are things always this exciting around here,

Aunt Tali?" Maisie suddenly appeared, looking over Tali's shoulder at her phone.

Tali angled the screen away, not wanting Maisie to see the bleeding victim behind her shop. She'd always felt protective of the girl, especially since her mom was so overbearing. Deanna and Rick had never exactly provided a happy home life.

Tali let out a long breath as she pondered Maisie's question. "I wish I could say they weren't. But in truth, yes. A most definite yes."

Maisie raised her eyebrows as if unsure how to respond. Finally, she said, "On a different note, this place looks great. I'm really excited for you. I mean, maybe I shouldn't say that, given the shooting and all. But I really wanted to come with my mom so she could surprise you. It's been too long."

Tali cast a grin at the girl. "Thank you, sweetie. I always love seeing you too."

She had more questions about Deanna and Maisie's sudden appearance here. But it didn't seem right to ask those right now.

She hoped she'd have time later.

She stepped away and squinted as she glanced at the phone screen again.

Was that Mac walking toward Cassidy?

He held his head and walked with a limp, his eyes glazed.

Something had happened to him, Tali realized. He'd been hurt.

Alarm raced through her.

At once, she forgot the instructions she'd been given.

Tali hurried outside, desperate to know if Mac was okay.

———

Mac looked up as someone rushed toward him.

Tali.

She paused in front of him, gripping his arms as she stared into his eyes. "Mac . . . what happened?"

He grumbled under his breath before shrugging. "Someone was on the fire escape waiting for me. When he saw me coming, he dropped a paint can on my head. Everything went black for a minute. Rookie mistake."

"What?" Tali gasped and tenderly touched the area where he held his head. "You need to be checked out."

Her concern warmed him—made him long for something he hadn't had in a long time.

A partner.

His wife had died nearly thirty years ago, and no other woman had turned his head since then.

No one until Tali.

He brought his thoughts back to the present. "I'll be okay."

"Mac . . ." Cassidy joined them, her gaze narrowed with concern over Mac. Then she sent Tali a look that clearly communicated her displeasure at Tali not following directions. "So much for staying inside . . ."

"I saw Mac on the video on my phone and—" Tali cut herself off as if she hadn't intended to say that. Her cheeks flushed.

Tali saw him on her phone?

She must have been watching the security camera footage.

Smart girl.

Law enforcement would need to see that footage soon.

Cassidy motioned to someone with the wave of her hand. "Hey, Peter, I need you over here."

One of the paramedics joined them and shone a light in Mac's eyes. Mac swatted him away, hating it when people made a fuss about him—especially when he wasn't trying to be the center of attention.

Peter shrugged and stepped back.

Mac went through the story with Cassidy about what had happened, concluding with, "He got away. I'm sorry."

"I sent Officer Dillinger to see if he could find the shooter too. So far, there's nothing. But we'll check for prints up on that fire escape as well."

"Good idea," Mac muttered.

Cassidy turned to Tali. "Do you have any idea who this guy is, Tali?"

Tali glanced back at the gunshot victim as paramedics put him on a gurney. She shook her head.

"I saw him in my shop and wondered who he was. But I don't think I've ever seen him before. Is he . . . ?" Tali appeared as if she wanted to say the word *dead*, but she couldn't bring herself to do so.

"He's still hanging on," Cassidy said. "We're going to Life Flight him to a hospital in Raleigh. The helicopter's on the way."

"What a nightmare." Tali rubbed her arms.

Mac wanted to step in, to offer her some comfort. But the whole situation had left him feeling off-kilter. His throbbing head didn't help.

Cassidy frowned as she looked back at the shop. "We're going to need to question everyone at the party. See if anyone recognizes this guy."

Tali nodded. "Of course."

But Mac didn't like where any of this was going, especially since Tali was involved . . . again.

CHAPTER 4

An hour had passed since the man had been shot.

Tali had been keeping an eye on the time as apprehension threatened to creep in and totally consume her. She'd heard Mac talking to Cassidy.

She'd heard them saying that the gunshot victim didn't have a wallet on him, so they didn't know his name yet.

He did have a phone in his pocket, however—one with a text message reading:

Meet me outside. Now. Or else.

Clearly, there was more to this story.

Cassidy and her team were still in the midst of

questioning everyone at the party to see if anyone recognized the man or knew anything.

So far, no one recognized him or had any clue about what was going on.

Which made this whole thing even more curious.

After each guest was questioned, Cassidy dismissed them to go home.

Tali made her way across the shop to Deanna, who stood alone. Maisie was on the other side of the shop, cleaning up some spilled coffee and reorganizing the sugar packets.

She was a woman after Tali's own heart.

The timing worked out because Tali had some questions for Deanna, who stood near the stairway absently sipping on her coffee while looking at her watch every few minutes.

It wasn't like her just to show up, especially since the trip from Georgia would need to be preplanned.

"Do you need somewhere to stay tonight?" Tali asked.

"No, we have a place. Thank you."

"What brings you here?" The more Tali thought about it, the more convinced she was that her sister-in-law and niece hadn't come for a simple visit.

"If you really want to know . . . Atlanta National is having a retreat here."

Everything seemed to freeze around Tali as she absorbed Deanna's words.

"What?" Certainly, she hadn't heard correctly.

Atlanta National was the bank her husband had worked for before he'd gone to prison. It was a smaller chain of banks—they had about thirty locations in Georgia, last she'd heard.

"You know we go on a retreat every year—the board of directors, that is," Deanna continued. "This year, they picked Lantern Beach."

Tali tried not to gawk. They'd come here, of all places?

That couldn't be a coincidence . . . right? "That's . . . interesting."

Deanna raised a finely penciled eyebrow. "Isn't it?"

Tali had more questions. But, before she could ask them, Cassidy approached.

At least the crowd had thinned out now.

"Can I finally see the picture of the dead man so I can leave?" Deanna interjected before Cassidy could say anything.

"He's not dead," Cassidy corrected, tucking a wavy blonde hair behind her ear. She looked casual tonight—more like a mom than a police chief. But she still held that fiercely determined look in her gaze. "The man was shot."

"Fine. Can I see a photo of this . . . *gunshot victim*?" Deanna asked the question with equal parts disdain and impatience.

Cassidy's gaze narrowed as if she didn't like the tone of Deanna's voice. Neither did Tali, for that matter.

Cassidy pulled the photo up on her phone and showed it to Deanna. "This is our guy."

Deanna glanced at the picture.

Her eyes widened.

She sucked in a breath.

That's when Tali realized that her sister-in-law knew something.

"Deanna?" Cassidy stared at her, picking up on her body language also.

"That's . . ." Deanna's hand went over her mouth, and she shook her head—all the airs she'd been putting on suddenly disappearing.

"Who is it?" Cassidy asked.

"That's Wesley Simmons."

"Simmons?" That was a name Tali hadn't heard in a long time. Certainly, it wasn't the same Simmons she'd known back in Georgia.

Deanna glanced at Tali. "Wesley Simmons . . . he's Arlo's son."

The air left Tali's lungs.

It couldn't be. Could it?

"You mean the CEO of Atlanta National?" Tali confirmed. "That Arlo?"

Deanna nodded, her hand remaining over her mouth. "Yes, one and the same. I can't believe his son has been shot . . . someone's going to need to let Arlo know. He's . . . he's here on the island now. For the retreat."

"Let us handle that." Cassidy's voice left no room for argument.

But Tali barely heard her.

Were her past and her present colliding here on Lantern Beach?

They couldn't be.

That would be too much of a coincidence.

Whatever was happening, she didn't like any of it.

————

Mac was standing near enough to hear most of Tali and Cassidy's conversation. He didn't consider it eavesdropping. He simply considered it a blessing to be in close enough proximity to overhear these things.

As soon as he'd heard Simmons, he *knew* the name sounded familiar.

Probably because Mac had been one of the investigators looking into a string of bank robberies down in Georgia thirty years ago. Mac and Tali hadn't realized their connection until after they'd struck up a friendship, when they'd begun to talk about their pasts.

He didn't like where this was going.

In fact, Wesley's father, Arlo, was the one who'd given the testimony that ultimately put Jimmy Robinson behind bars. He'd claimed Jimmy was working odd hours, acting strangely, and that the bonus check he'd received hadn't been authorized by the bank.

Jimmy was Tali's husband. But the man had died while in prison serving a sentence for his role in the deadly bank robberies.

Mac resisted the urge to move closer to Tali.

The two of them had come a long way since they'd initially met. But they still had issues they needed to talk through. Namely the fact that Mac had helped put Tali's husband in prison.

To this day, she remained firm that her husband was innocent of his charges. Mac had no doubt part of Tali blamed Mac for the grief and loss she'd experienced while her husband was locked up. Mac knew Tali had wanted children but, because of her faithfulness to her vows, she'd remained married—and therefore childless.

As Cassidy stepped away to talk to Dillinger a minute—probably about making a visit to Wesley's father—Tali started looking through security camera footage with Officer Leggott.

Mac's gaze traveled to Deanna. Her phone buzzed and, as she glanced at the screen, her face paled.

Mac squinted.

What was that about?

Something Deanna had seen on the phone had shaken her up.

Did it have something to do with Wesley?

But now he was more curious than ever.

A would-be killer roamed the streets. Even though Deanna had been inside when it happened, she was still one of the few people on the island who actually knew Wesley. That made her a person of interest.

There was more to this story.

Mac was going to find out what.

CHAPTER 5

Tali had just finished finding the security footage Cassidy requested when she saw Mac approaching.

But he wasn't looking at her.

His gaze was on Deanna, who stood near the window.

Serena had left around twenty minutes ago—after Cassidy questioned her—and now there was no one to distract Deanna and Maisie.

Maisie held Sugar as she perused books in the science fiction section. Maisie had always loved Sugar.

In fact, Tali had always thought of Maisie as the daughter she'd never had. The two had spent a lot of time together when Maisie was young. They still kept in touch, though not as much as Tali would like.

"What message did you just get on your phone?" Mac demanded as he stared at Deanna.

His voice drew Tali's attention.

Deanna's eyebrows shot up, and she quickly stuffed her phone back into her purse. "I don't know what you're talking about."

"I just saw you read a message." He frowned as he stared at her. "You looked as if you'd seen a ghost."

Deanna raised her chin with annoyance. "I don't think that's any of your business."

Mac placed his hands on his hips. "A man connected with *you* was shot outside a bookstore where *you* just happened to be. I'd say it *is* our business."

Deanna's gaze narrowed, and she tilted her head back in an almost "How dare you question me" look. "That's awfully presumptuous of you."

Tali stepped closer, partly as an intermediary and partly because she wanted to know what was going on. "Deanna, if you don't have anything to hide then I don't see what the big deal is about sharing whatever it was you saw on your phone."

Deanna's gaze went to Tali, and anger simmered in the depths of her eyes. She certainly didn't like Tali taking Mac's side, did she? The fact didn't surprise Tali.

"I hope everybody on this island isn't as pushy as you." She sneered at Mac one more time, almost as if for good measure. "If you must know, I did get a rather disturbing text. But it wasn't about Wesley Simmons. It was about something . . . personal."

Mac crossed his arms, unable to hide his annoyance. "Then what was it about?"

Deanna's mouth dropped open. "You just don't give up, do you?"

"All you have to do is answer the question, and then I'll drop it. But if you'd like, I can call Police Chief Chambers over. I'm sure she could be more convincing—"

Deanna gave Mac another icy glare before slowly conceding. "Okay, fine. Although, I don't like feeling as if I'm a suspect." She glanced at Tali, sending a silent message, before turning back to Mac. "But this is for your eyes only."

Tali shrugged and stepped away—but only after Mac saw a look of hurt on her face.

Deanna showed Mac her phone.

What he saw there wasn't what he expected.

It was a reminder about an upcoming medical appointment with a neurologist.

Deanna looked up at him and lowered her voice. "Please . . . you can't tell anyone—not until I let my daughter know."

———

Mac waited at Tali's place until everyone else had left.

Everyone but Tali and Cassidy.

Paper coffee cups and leftover pastries had been abandoned on several surfaces. Chairs weren't arranged as neatly as they'd once been. The music was off, and a deflated feeling filled the air.

The grand opening had turned into a nightmare.

Now, all people would remember was the man who'd been shot.

Tali turned toward Cassidy, trepidation on her face as she held Sugar against her chest. "Is this where you tell me not to leave the island?"

After everything she'd been through, Mac couldn't blame her thinking in worst-case scenarios. Life had given her a bad hand, but Tali had handled her circumstances with a grace and dignity Mac admired.

Cassidy offered a compassionate half smile/half frown. "No, you're not a suspect. Numerous witnesses, including me, saw you inside the bookstore when the shooting occurred. But I do worry about you, Tali."

Mac expected Tali to look relieved, but her shoulders remained tense.

"You don't think this is linked with me or the bookstore, do you?" Tali's gaze narrowed as she waited for Cassidy's answer.

"I wouldn't . . ." Cassidy frowned, almost as if she didn't want to finish the statement. "Except for the fact you have a past connection with the man who was shot."

"I agree that it does seem coincidental."

Mac could tell this situation was beginning to get to Tali. Her stiff posture, the way she rubbed her neck and temples, the tight lines on her face . . . she was feeling the stress from this.

Mac knew the solution: he had to help her find answers.

He turned to Cassidy. "What's next?"

"We're going to continue looking for this gunman."

"What did the security camera footage show?" he asked.

Cassidy frowned. "Unfortunately, it showed a Dementor creeping around the building."

He narrowed his eyes, certain he hadn't heard correctly. "A Dementor?"

"From Harry Potter," Tali said. "You know? They're the dark creatures who inhabit the wizarding world. You not a Harry Potter fan?"

"Not my cup of tea."

Cassidy examined Mac's head with narrowed eyes. "We're going to need to keep an eye on that injury of yours. I called Doc Clemson, and he said you might have a concussion."

"I'm fine." Mac waved Cassidy off again.

She rolled her eyes to the side. "That's what you always say."

"Because it's always the truth. I'm always fine. I'm still alive, aren't I?"

"Mac . . . one day all these things might catch up with you. We can't let that happen." Cassidy gently laid her hand on his arm. "You know you're like a father to me."

He was fond of Cassidy also and thought of her as family. "And I appreciate that. But you don't need to worry about me. You have enough other things to worry about . . . and I'm not only talking about these cases you're working. I'm talking about that precious little girl of yours also."

Her eyes lit with warmth. "Did I tell you Faith just started crawling?"

"She did?" Mac raised his eyebrows. "I knew she was an overachiever—just like her mom and dad."

"Life just got a lot busier for me and Ty."

Ty was Cassidy's husband and a former Navy SEAL who now ran two organizations on the island

—a private security group and a program called Hope House that helped wounded veterans.

As Cassidy, Mac, and Tali talked, Officer Dillinger walked back into the bookstore and held up something in a plastic evidence bag. "Look what I just found."

Mac sucked in a breath.

A gun.

"Is that the weapon used to shoot Mr. Simmons?" Cassidy asked, even though they all knew the answer. She stepped closer for a better look.

"Hard to say for sure, but it seems like a good guess." Dillinger nodded slowly. "It was in a trash can about two blocks from here. We'll run prints on it, of course."

"Why do I have a feeling you have more to say?" Cassidy squinted as she stared at Dillinger.

"I went ahead and ran the serial numbers through the system. We already got a hit."

Cassidy's eyebrows shot up. "Is that right? Do tell."

"The gun belongs to a man named Allan Warwick."

"Chewy . . ." Tali muttered.

She blinked as she seemed to realize everyone was listening—and confused about her statement.

"That's Allan's nickname," she explained. "He works for Atlanta National . . ."

CHAPTER 6

First thing the next morning, Mac went right to the police station to talk to Cassidy. He hadn't slept all night—mostly because Doc Clemson, one of his best friends, had told him that he shouldn't since he may have a concussion.

Mac would say he was tired, but he'd had four cups of coffee already this morning, and now he felt wired.

He wasn't going to tell Doc Clemson about the coffee because then he might get a lecture. Too much caffeine tended to make his heart race and cause insomnia. Doc Clemson had been on his case for a while about that. Less caffeine, more sleep, lots of vegetables.

"You look surprisingly bright-eyed and bushy-tailed," Cassidy said when Mac walked into her office and handed her some coffee.

She paused from looking over some reports and lifted the cup to her lips.

"Aren't I always?" Mac raised his own cup and took a sip. "I might as well be a squirrel collecting acorns."

"Halloween is coming up . . . might work out well as a costume for you."

He had other ideas for Halloween.

Besides, even though he was sixty-eight, he still considered himself spry. He intended on keeping it that way for a long time. Being this age, at one time, had seemed so old.

But it seemed like just yesterday he was in his thirties. Most of the time, Mac didn't feel much different. It was only when life threw him into a tail-spin—like unfavorable doctor's reports or when friends passed from this life entirely too early—that he remembered his age and fallibility.

"You know why I'm here." He sat down in the chair across from her. "Any updates you can tell me about?"

Cassidy straightened the folders on her desk. "Mr. Simmons made it through the night. He's in a coma in the hospital in Raleigh. The doctor said he'd call if there were any updates."

"Did you arrest Chewy?" Mac remembered the man well.

He was tall and thin, with thick glasses and a wide smile . . . the real life-of-the-party type. His thick, messy hair earned him the nickname—as well as the hair on his arms, back, and neck.

She let out a long breath. "We brought him in last night. He reported the gun missing a week ago—we verified that. Said he'd had a party at his house and was showing off his gun collection. When he went back to his cabinet the next day, one of the weapons was gone."

"Who was at this party?"

"The board members, amongst others."

"Interesting."

"He said Wesley was like a son to him. He seemed upset over what had happened—and shaken. Because he reported the gun missing, we can't hold him. Plus, he has an alibi during the shooting."

"Any other updates?"

She let out a long breath. "We also talked to Wesley Simmons's father last night. Arlo was upset, of course."

"Is he heading out this morning?" No ferries ran from the island at night—although someone like Arlo Simmons could easily afford alternate transportation.

"He said he's going to stick around a while longer

since his son isn't awake yet." A critical edge tinged Cassidy's voice, one that most wouldn't hear unless they knew her well.

Her own parents were wealthy and had often chosen work over her. If anyone had the right to form an opinion about a situation like this, it was Cassidy.

That made Mac wonder just how close Arlo and his son were.

Arlo Simmons had never given Mac warm, fuzzy feelings, to say the least.

When Mac had talked to him during the investigation in Atlanta, the man had spoken with clipped words and never dropped his business persona—even after two people had died during robberies in banks he owned.

Mac hadn't been impressed.

"What about this other guy on the board? Perry Johnson?" Mac asked. "I did a little research on the board members last night. I mean, I assume this shooting has something to do with this retreat."

"I do too. But we both know that assumptions can get us in trouble. Perry Johnson is new to the whole Atlanta National scene. I haven't found any evidence that would link him to those bank robberies so we can probably rule him out. In fact, he's from Florida."

"So we have a man visiting Lantern Beach from Georgia who was shot behind a bookstore/coffeeshop during the grand opening," Mac muttered. "The only people on the island he knew besides Tali were those who came with him for this corporate retreat. Am I tracking so far?"

Cassidy sighed. "Tracking like a hurricane."

"Exactly how many people came on this retreat?"

"Only eight. As you know, Lantern Beach isn't exactly set up for big corporate events. Apparently, the operating board takes a trip to various locations every year. This year, they decided to come here."

Mac let out a grunt, wondering about the timing of that—especially since Tali had recently moved here. "I take it Wesley Simmons is on the board."

"He's chief operations officer. Even stranger than that, it was his idea to come to Lantern Beach." Cassidy shrugged. "That's what Arlo said, at least."

Now *that* was interesting.

The more Mac learned, the less he liked this.

Why would Wesley want to come here when there were other places with much nicer, all-inclusive resorts with endless amenities?

He studied Cassidy's placid expression. "Do you think that was a coincidence?"

"It seems like too much, doesn't it?"

"It's definitely curious. Tali said Wesley was acting weird during the bookstore opening. I'm wondering if he chose Lantern Beach because he knew she was here. Maybe he even wanted to talk to her."

"But what would he want to talk to her about?"

Mac let out a long breath. "I'm wondering if Wesley might know something about those bank robberies. Maybe something has been weighing on his mind all these years. Thirty years ago, he would have been around fifteen—old enough to pick up on things."

"Sounds plausible." Cassidy shifted. "I did go through Wesley's phone. There were other threatening messages—things like 'Talk and you'll die,' 'Don't blow this now,' 'I know what you're up to.'"

"So, this guy probably realized Wesley was thinking about talking and wanted to silence him."

"That's my guess."

Mac glanced at his watch.

It was time to meet Tali for breakfast.

They'd set this date last week.

They were finally going to talk through what happened thirty years ago.

Now it seemed more urgent than ever that they find some resolution.

———

Tali had hardly slept all night.

Her restlessness wasn't necessarily because she'd felt in danger—even though she might be.

She just had too many thoughts rushing through her head.

Every time she took a deep breath and felt peace about making the right decision by moving here to Lantern Beach, something else happened. A crime. A death.

Maybe she'd been a hardhead. Maybe this was all God's way of saying she should have never come here, but she'd been too dense to notice the signs.

Tali didn't think of herself as being dense. In fact, she knew she was smart. She was practically an expert at researching and tracking down information. She'd organized uncountable successful events as a librarian. And she loved listening to others, which she considered a sign of intelligence. Her mom had always said that, at least.

But four different crimes connected with her within four months of living here? That should tell Tali something.

However, she had come this far . . .

She sighed and took one more glance at herself in the bathroom mirror to make sure she looked okay.

She appeared tired, but tired was the new energetic—at her age, at least.

Even though yesterday had been the official

grand opening, Tali was only going to keep this place open on the weekends right now. She still had to find people to help staff it, and she was learning the ropes about being a business owner.

Tali thought it would be better if she slowly eased herself into this rather than jumping in with both feet.

She gave Sugar a pat on the head and set him on the floor before grabbing her purse from the kitchen counter. "I'll be gone two or three hours. You'll be okay here by yourself, right, boy?"

Sugar barked up at her and wagged his tail.

Tali had been tempted to cancel on Mac this morning. But they'd put off this conversation for far too long.

Tali didn't want to open this can of worms.

So someone else had opened it for her.

With one more glance at Sugar, Tali left her apartment, which was located directly over the bookstore.

Several people were on the boardwalk as she stepped out, continuing on with their day as if nothing had happened last night.

She wondered about the blood behind her building. Was it still there? Would people see it and wonder what had happened? Would they assume it was a grisly Halloween decoration? Or had word about the shooting already spread all over the island?

Her guess was that the last choice was the correct one. News spread quickly in small towns like Lantern Beach.

She patted the skeleton sitting on a bench by her front door—dubbed Starvin' Marvin by Doc Clemson —as she stepped outside. The wind was especially sharp and cold today. Often, she walked to The Crazy Chefette, the restaurant where she and Mac were meeting.

But she wasn't up for the stroll right now. Instead, she headed to the lot down the street and climbed into her car.

A few minutes later, she pulled into the parking area of the restaurant, automatically scanning the lot for Mac's vehicle.

He was already here.

Tali's nerves kicked in and, as she climbed from her Volkswagen Bug, she drew in a deep breath.

Perhaps she was delaying the inevitable—even if only by a couple of seconds.

As she started around her car toward the sidewalk leading to The Crazy Chefette, she looked up and saw a dark-colored sedan headed down the road —going entirely too fast and veering over the lines.

Was the driver distracted? Had he or she reached down to grab their phone? To quiet a crying child in the backseat?

Tali didn't know. But she froze, unable to move.

Instead, she watched as the vehicle continued to careen toward her.

That's when she realized the driver wasn't distracted.

The driver was purposefully aiming straight for her.

CHAPTER 7

Mac glanced out the window, waiting for Tali to arrive.

A small smile tugged at his lips when he saw her bright yellow Volkswagen Beetle pull into the back of the parking lot.

He watched as Tali stepped out wearing jeans and a brown and teal flannel shirt. Her blonde hair blew with the breeze as she heaved her oversized basket-weave purse onto her shoulder.

As always, she was a sight to see—and someone who always made his pulse race.

She started walking toward the sidewalk. Then she froze.

Her gaze fixated on something in the distance.

Her shoulders tightened as if anticipating the worst.

Mac stood from his seat and paced toward the front door.

What was she looking at? He followed her gaze.

That's when he saw the dark-colored vehicle racing toward Tali.

She was like a deer in the headlights as she stood staring at it.

As his adrenaline surged, he dashed outside.

"Tali!" he yelled, trying to break her out of her trance.

She glanced at him.

"Move!" He knew he couldn't reach her in time, but he ran toward her anyway. "Get out of the way!"

With mere seconds to spare, she lunged around the vehicle and dove onto the ground. Her eyes closed as her body slammed into the asphalt.

Meanwhile, the driver swerved, barely missing Tali and the Volkswagen before squealing away.

As it did, Mac committed the license plate to memory.

Whoever did this wasn't going to get away with it. Mac would make sure of it.

But right now, his first concern was Tali.

He rushed toward her and knelt on the ground. "Are you okay, honey?"

Honey? The word had slipped out.

Tali didn't seem to notice.

She sat up, looking dazed as people filed from the restaurant to check things out.

Mac saw the scrapes on her hands. She shifted again, and he saw the rip in her jeans as well.

Tali examined her hands and frowned as she looked at her wounds. "All things considered, I guess I'm okay. I'm not dead."

And she wouldn't be if Mac had any control over it.

But someone had clearly been trying to send a message.

She looked up and blanched as if just noticing the crowd around her. Mac recognized a couple people from church and one of the contractors Tali had hired.

Lisa Dillinger, who owned the restaurant, and her cousin, Cadence Garth, knelt beside Tali as others stood close by.

"I can get you something to clean that up with." Lisa frowned when she saw the cuts on Tali's hands. "Unless you prefer to go to the clinic."

"Maybe that's not a bad idea." Mac took Tali's arm and carefully helped her to her feet.

Cadence scooped up the items that had tumbled from Tali's purse and tossed them back inside.

"You all stop making a fuss over me." Tali waved her hand in the air as if shooing them. "I'm fine."

"You could've been killed." Lisa frowned. "I saw it all happening from the restaurant."

"When you're younger and you fall, people laugh at you," Tali muttered. "But when you get old and fall, everyone's concerned. I would prefer you all laugh right now."

"Unfortunately, this is no laughing matter." Mac's voice held no amusement. "Someone just tried to run over you."

"But they didn't," Tali reminded everyone.

Mac frowned and rubbed his stiff, tight jaw. It brought him no pleasure to say his next words. But he said them anyway.

"That doesn't mean they're not going to try again to kill you," he reminded her.

Tali glanced up at him as his words hung in the air, an ominous truth no one could deny.

———

Tali hated that everyone was making a fuss about her. Really, this whole thing was just embarrassing.

At the same time, she appreciated their concern. No one was trying to humiliate her . . . they were only trying to help.

She glanced at the crowd around her, trying to figure out how to politely send them away. "Thank you all, but I'm fine. More than anything, I'd just like to get inside, get a good cup of coffee, and order some of those pumpkin waffles before Lisa runs out."

Everyone around her dispersed, talking amongst themselves. Then Mac took hold of one arm and Lisa the other, and they led her inside. Tali ignored the stares of restaurant patrons as she was escorted to a booth in the corner.

One cup of coffee already sat on the table—no doubt it was Mac's. As soon as she was seated, Lisa scurried away and brought Tali her own cup—fixed just like she liked it, with cream and sugar. She'd even added some whip.

Tali felt the woman's concerned gaze on her.

"Are you sure you don't want me to call Doc?" Lisa frowned.

"I'm fine," Tali insisted. "I promise."

Lisa finally nodded. "Well, I won't stand here and stare at you, but if you need anything you know where we are."

"Thank you, and I appreciate that."

Once it was just Tali and Mac, her shoulders loosened slightly.

"That was . . . unexpected." She meant the words to sound casual, but they didn't.

Mac narrowed his eyes and glanced at his phone as he typed something. "I'm letting Cassidy know what happened so she can be on the lookout for that car."

"Did you get a license plate number?"

"I sure did."

"That's good, at least," Tali said, although she wasn't surprised.

Mac was usually on top of these things. Police work seemed to be in his blood.

She gave her coffee a little stir, trying to ignore the stinging from her wounds. No doubt she'd be sore from the jarring impact as well.

"You really should get those scrapes cleaned up." Mac glanced at her hands and frowned again.

Tali studied her palms and saw the raw skin there. "I suppose I should. But I'll be fine for a minute. I just need to collect myself. Besides, ripped jeans are all the rage, right? I probably look younger now."

She felt Mac's gaze lingering on her. The truth was, she *was* shaken. That driver had almost run her over.

On purpose.

She was certain of it.

The driver hadn't seemed distracted. In fact, he'd seemed to be looking right at her.

She was fairly certain a man had been behind the wheel. However, it was hard to say for sure. The bad news was that she couldn't see his face. The windows were tinted so all she could make out was a faint outline.

She took another sip of her drink and noticed her hands still trembled. The tremors gave away her inner turmoil.

Mac reached across the table and covered her hand with his. "It's okay to admit that you're shaken."

Tali stared at him a moment before looking away, fighting a surge of embarrassment. "I know."

The truth was, she'd been on her own for so long that she was used to watching out for herself. Sure, she had friends and neighbors and her church community. But mostly she'd been alone. With Jimmy behind bars, she'd had no other choice but to take care of herself.

She let out a long breath. This was all too, too much.

The hits just kept coming. When would they end?

As a surge of apprehension rose in her, she stood.

"I'm going to run to the restroom," she murmured. "I'll wash off these cuts. Just give me a few minutes."

Mac nodded.

But Tali knew that the main reason she needed to step away was so she could gather herself and her emotions before she faced Mac again . . . especially if they were going to have "the" conversation—the one she'd been dreading ever since she learned about his connection to her husband, Jimmy.

CHAPTER 8

As Mac waited for Tali, he kept one eye on his phone and one eye on the front door of the restaurant.

If someone had purposefully tried to run Tali over, there was a chance this person might try something else.

He had to make sure that didn't happen.

He was also monitoring his phone in case Cassidy got back with him about that license plate number.

She was heading to the restaurant now to take a statement from Tali. Last night's crime was somehow connected with Tali, and Mac had to wonder how this Atlanta National retreat tied in with her past and her present.

Finally, Tali emerged from the bathroom. Gauze

stretched across her hands. Lisa must have caught her and helped bandage her wounds.

Shortly after, Cassidy arrived and took Tali's statement.

After Cassidy left, Tali turned to Mac, her expression downtrodden and heavy. "This wasn't the way I wanted to start my day."

"I know we were going to meet so we could talk about . . ." He swallowed hard as he paused, unable to finish his statement out of concern for her emotional well-being. "But I understand after everything that's happened that you might not want to—"

"No, it's okay. We need to talk. We've put this conversation off for far too long."

Mac's gut twisted. It wasn't often he felt nervous.

But in this situation, he did.

Based on the way this discussion went, it could be a real turning point for his relationship with Tali.

A turning point that could draw them closer.

Or a turning point that could drive them apart.

———

"I don't even know where to start." Tali glanced at the coffee in front of her, her heart suddenly burdened.

She'd ordered her favorite pumpkin waffles with

warm compote, honey anglaise, and fresh whipped cream. Normally, this meal would cheer her up.

Right now, she wasn't sure.

Talking about what had happened with Jimmy was one of her least favorite topics of conversation. Too many bad memories had to be relived each time. Too much heartache.

"I know it's cliché, but I suppose we could start from the beginning." Mac shrugged and glanced at his plate—two eggs over easy, two pieces of bacon, hashbrowns, and toast.

He'd barely touched his food either.

They could pretend like everything was normal, but nothing was.

"But where is the beginning, really? It's just such a long, winding, twisted mess." Tali ran her thumb across the lip of her cheerful orange coffee mug.

"I agree. Would it help if I started?"

Some of the pressure left her shoulders at the idea of Mac taking the lead. "Okay."

However, Tali had a feeling she knew *exactly* what he would say—nothing she wanted to hear.

He frowned and ran a hand over his mouth before starting. "I know you've believed for all these years that Jimmy was innocent and wrongly sentenced to prison."

She didn't bother to respond. Mac clearly knew that was her stance.

"But I hoped I might be able to explain my side of this to you," he continued, the normal sparkle leaving his gaze.

Tali wasn't sure if she wanted to hear this at all. Nor was she sure that she would learn anything now that she hadn't learned during the trial. Hadn't all the proof been laid out there? She knew Mac well enough to know he hadn't been sitting on information for all these years.

"This all started with a bank robbery at the Atlanta National location in downtown Atlanta," Mac said. "Four masked robbers were involved, and more than one hundred thousand dollars was stolen."

Tali nodded, his statement seeming safe enough. "Correct."

"The police thought it was an isolated robbery. But, over the course of the next two months, there were four more robberies involving the same four men. Nearly a million dollars had been stolen at that point."

"Also correct." The crime had dominated headlines and made people in the area live in fear.

But here was where the story would take a turn for the worse.

Tali braced herself for what Mac would say next.

A frown flickered on his lips before he continued. "It was during the sixth robbery that things took a deadly turn. One of the bank's armed guards was shot and later died at the hospital."

Tali frowned as the memories rushed back. She only wished she hadn't had a front row seat in all this. She hadn't known the guard, yet she'd grieved for the man's family.

So much pain, and all for what? Some money that these guys wanted to steal instead of earn?

It was a shame in so many ways.

"Then there was another robbery—no casualties," Tali finished. "The eighth bank heist was where a teller was killed. She was fresh out of college and going to get married in three months. Jillian Douglas died at the scene."

"Correct." He shifted in his seat and frowned.

As bad as those details were, Tali knew that there was much more to the story.

"After the sixth robbery, we got some intel that led us to a man named Robbie Long," Mac continued. "We watched him and determined he might be one of the robbers. He had two good friends who were on our suspect list also. We didn't know who the fourth guy might be."

"And you also assumed at that time that there

was an inside man who worked for the bank—essentially, a fifth man, a silent partner."

He nodded slowly. "That's right. *Someone* was feeding these guys information about the layout of the banks, about how security worked there, about where most of the cash was kept, about codes to the vault. Not everyone working at the banks knew that information—only certain members of upper management."

"Like Jimmy." Tali frowned.

"Like Jimmy . . . Jimmy who just happened to be seen talking to two of the suspects ten days before the first robbery occurred."

Her gut twisted. "He said those boys asked to meet with him to talk about a career in finance. They were in college and needed to do an interview for a project. At the time, Jimmy said he felt honored that they'd even talked to him about being a mentor."

"Or that could have just been Jimmy's excuse. Believe me—it brings me no pleasure to say those words."

Tali frowned again and crossed her arms. "That's all circumstantial. Those college boys could've been setting him up!"

"Clearly, they weren't looking for career advice. They were art majors."

Tali bristled. She'd been down this road too many times already.

This conversation was getting them nowhere.

Mac's mind was made up, and nothing Tali said would change that.

She resisted a sigh.

So why were they even trying?

CHAPTER 9

Mac could sense he was losing Tali. This conversation wasn't going the direction he hoped. Instead, he felt the wall between them growing higher and higher.

He took a sip of his coffee, using the brief moment to collect his thoughts.

"Jimmy would've told me if he'd been a part of this." Tali's voice rose with emotion.

"But he did tell you right before he was arrested that he'd gotten some extra money so you guys could take a vacation and start a family."

Her gaze narrowed. "That doesn't mean he got those funds via an illegal means."

"So money just showed up in his account?"

"It was a bonus!" Tali's voice rose emphatically.

She seemed to realize her increasing volume, and her shoulders slumped.

Mac drew a deep breath and slowly released it. "Jimmy's boss—Arlo Simmons—told us they hadn't given out the bonus."

Tali crossed her arms. "What if Arlo was lying?"

"Why would he lie?"

"Maybe someone else at the top was part of this and, in order to cover up their own involvement, they framed my husband. That's why he'd lie!"

Mac stared at her. Tali really believed that was what had happened. He saw the loyalty in her gaze.

He didn't want to crush that. Didn't want to ruin the reputation of her deceased husband. Mostly, he didn't want Tali to hate him.

But the truth was unavoidable.

"Did Jimmy tell you that we questioned him several times before we made the arrest?"

Tali's eyes widened. "What?"

Mac nodded somberly, not enjoying telling her this. "We did. He had to know it was coming."

"But . . . that can't be true." Her voice dropped, and betrayal filled her gaze.

"My goal was always to follow the evidence," Mac said quietly, not wanting to upset her any more than she already was.

"But what if the evidence was wrong?" Tali's gaze latched onto his as she waited for his response.

"How could the evidence be wrong in this case?" The question seemed simple enough.

Tali crossed her arms, her waffles untouched and growing as cold as her expression. "I know how this works. The police needed to close the case. There was mounting pressure from city leaders. Public scrutiny. The whole area was on edge. So the police zeroed in on Jimmy—you zeroed in on him—and went after him."

Mac drew in a quick breath, nearly feeling as if he'd been slapped. "We also looked into other people at Atlanta National. None of them made sense."

Tali's gaze remained defiant and stubborn. "I still stand by my statement that all the evidence was circumstantial. Nothing directly linked my husband to those robbers. Just because he met with those two college boys didn't mean anything. Those guys set him up, knowing Jimmy would be an easy scapegoat."

"You know what they say, though . . . follow the money."

"But maybe you were following a trail that someone else set up, one that was meant to distract you." Agitation lingered beneath her otherwise calm tone. "Someone gave that money to him to frame him. This person either worked at the bank or was able to hack into their system to arrange the deposit."

Mac hesitated before saying, "Jimmy knew it was coming, Tali. He was expecting that money."

"Because it was a bonus from Atlanta National."

Mac stared at her another moment, wanting to refute her statement.

But there was no use trying to change her mind.

Tali raised her chin. "Jimmy had worked his way up from banker to asset manager, to loan officer, and then management. He had a good salary. A promising future. Why would he want to mess that up? What you seem to be discounting is the fact Jimmy had no motive. He had more to lose than he had to gain."

Tali almost sounded like a lawyer making her closing argument—and she was very convincing.

Before Mac could respond, the door to the restaurant opened, and a vaguely familiar man stepped inside.

He was probably close to Mac's age, and he had a head full of thick white hair and a squarish build—from his jaw to his shoulders. Mac didn't know much about designer clothing, but he would bet that's what the man was wearing. Something about the stranger screamed *affluent*.

The man glanced around as if looking for a table.

Then his gaze stopped on Tali.

His eyes narrowed as he stormed toward her.

Mac tensed as he prepared himself to act, to protect her if necessary.

The man paused by the table and glared at Tali. "My son is in the hospital, and it's all your fault!"

———

Tali felt the air leave her lungs as she stared at Arlo Simmons.

She drew in a deep breath and reminded herself to keep her composure—reminded herself that the man was probably grieving, and that pain could make people act out. "Arlo . . . I had nothing to do with what happened yesterday."

"Then why was *my* son at *your* little bookstore?"

Tali tilted her chin higher. "That's what the police would also like to know. Wesley didn't speak with me, and I didn't invite him. I didn't know who he was until . . . until after he'd been shot."

Arlo's eyes narrowed as his nostrils flared. "This was all your master plan, wasn't it?"

She drew in a sharp breath. "How could it be my master plan? I didn't even know you all were going to be on the island."

His glare deepened. "I'm betting you worked it

out to have the retreat here. You somehow manipulated Wesley into choosing Lantern Beach. You wanted to get us all here so you could exact revenge on the bank as payback for your husband."

Tali gasped.

Mac stood, his hands on his hips. "Your accusations are unnecessary. You need to apologize. Right now."

Arlo stepped closer to Mac, not backing down as anger consumed him. "I don't have anything to apologize for. This is all just another nightmare. And guess who's at the center of it again? A Robinson."

Tali felt her heart beating faster. This couldn't be happening.

But it was.

She glanced around. Everyone in the restaurant had gone silent, and all eyes were on them. She grabbed Mac's arm and tugged him back down into his seat.

"It's okay," she murmured. "Arlo is just upset because his son was hurt."

"Of course I'm upset because my son's been hurt!" Arlo threw his hands in the air, his rage as strong as ever. The man was known for having a temper, but usually he tried to hide it. Not right now.

Tali's words hadn't calmed him in the least.

"You're going to pay for this!" Arlo glared at Tali. "Do you understand?"

Tali could hardly breathe.

She said nothing.

But she heard his threat loud and clear.

CHAPTER 10

Tali still felt stunned, even after Arlo stormed from the restaurant.

If he'd come here to eat, he'd apparently lost his appetite.

She glanced around and noticed everyone still staring at her.

Why wouldn't they be? Arlo had caused quite the scene.

Her pulse continued to race.

For years, she'd wondered if anything would have turned out differently if she'd confronted Arlo and his cronies all those years ago. She felt certain one of them knew more than they let on. One of them might have even been the one to set up Jimmy.

Instead, Tali had remained polite, waiting for the justice system to do its job.

She'd been so sure the truth would eventually come to the surface.

That Jimmy wouldn't be convicted on circumstantial evidence.

But the justice system had failed her.

Had failed Jimmy.

"I would love nothing more than to go after that guy," Mac muttered, the scowl seeming frozen on his face.

"He's just upset." But was that all there was to it?

Arlo had never been one of Tali's favorite people. Jimmy hadn't liked him either. But Jimmy had put up with Arlo since the man was his boss.

"Do you want to leave?" Mac stared at her from across the table.

Tali thought about it a moment before shaking her head. "No, I'd really like to finish my breakfast . . . and our conversation. But before we do, do you think it's odd that Arlo was here instead of with Wesley at the hospital?"

"I thought of that." Mac frowned. "I do think that it's a little strange. If I had kids and one of them was on life support, I would be there with them."

Tali closed her eyes. "I did hear something sometime about an ugly divorce between Arlo and his wife. I suppose that could have something to do with this situation. If I have the chance, I'll ask Deanna about that."

"Do you and Deanna have a very close relationship?"

Tali shrugged. "We've never been the best of friends. I always wanted to be, but we just never connected like that. We come at life from two different perspectives, and I don't believe in forcing relationships that just aren't meant to be."

"What is she like?"

Tali let out a breath and picked at her waffle, which looked cold and tasteless now. "She's . . . well, I suppose most people see her as being snobby and condescending. She married Jimmy's younger brother, who passed away about eight years ago from cancer. She seems to have grown more bitter over the years. I've been really close to Maisie—Deanna's daughter—ever since she was born. She's more like Jimmy—down-to-earth and kind."

"In other words, not like her mother." Mac unapologetically raised an eyebrow.

Tali shrugged, not denying his statement. "I suppose you could say that. I did text the two of them this morning, and they're going to come over for dinner this evening. Maybe I can find out more information then."

"That could be a good idea."

She took another sip of her coffee, which had also gotten cold. She didn't even care right now.

Tali finally pulled her gaze back up to Mac's. They'd strayed from their earlier conversation—the entire reason they'd met—but still had no real conclusion.

She didn't want to walk away leaving so many things open-ended. That had been happening for too long now.

Finally, she let out a breath. "I'm not really sure where we stand, Mac."

Mac's gaze locked with hers. "That's up to you, Tali."

At the kindness in his voice, moisture rushed to her eyes. Maybe it was Mac's statement. Or maybe it was everything happening right now.

Tali wasn't sure.

But she wasn't normally one to feel this rush of emotions.

Her gaze fluttered back up to meet Mac's. "Why did you have to be the one to arrest my husband?"

He stared at her a moment, an unreadable look in his blue eyes.

What was he thinking right now? That Tali was a poor sap who believed in her husband, even when all the evidence was stacked against him? That Mac could never be with someone who so blindly believed in a man he felt was guilty?

She had no idea, but she waited to hear what he had to say.

Finally, Mac leaned across the table and lowered his voice. "How about if I look into what happened again?"

Everything around her seemed to freeze at his words.

Tali wasn't sure if she'd understood him correctly. "Say that again?"

"I can look into those bank robberies. Give the evidence another once-over. I'm not sure what will come of it, but I'd be more than happy to—"

"You would do that for me?" Tali sounded breathless, even to her own ears.

Mac nodded slowly, almost as if her reaction had confused him. "Of course, I would, Tali. But I'm afraid the results might be the same."

Maybe they would be.

But maybe they wouldn't.

———

An hour later, Mac was back in his office.

He was officially the mayor of Lantern Beach. Once he'd given up the job as police chief, he'd tried to enjoy retirement. But he found that wasn't really possible. He liked to be involved.

When a conniving, manipulative man had run for mayoral office, Mac had known he couldn't let that guy be elected.

That's when Mac had run for mayor, and here he was more than two years later. The job had stuck, and he felt right at home in this position.

On an island this size, he wasn't busy all the time. The bustle seemed to come in spurts.

The next island event was the Lantern Beach Fall Festival in three days. He'd preside over the island's costume contest. It was a Lantern Beach tradition and always fun—except when there was a demented, costumed gunman running around.

But right now, not much was on Mac's schedule, which worked in his favor.

He used a few of his contacts to find the information he needed. The process had been relatively painless. Then he began reviewing everything that had been sent to him.

As Mac watched footage from the first bank robbery, details flashed back to him.

What really bugged him was the fact that the fourth robber had escaped justice. None of the men who were currently behind bars, despite the plea deals offered to them, had given up the identity of their fourth team member.

This guy just happened to be the one who'd pulled the trigger in both of the homicides connected with the robberies.

Three decades ago, security cameras weren't as prevalent, and the footage that was available tended to be grainy and gray. But banks were one of the few organizations to tap into this type of technology.

Today, a criminal could hardly do anything without being caught on camera. Crime was riskier in that regard, he supposed.

Mac paused the old video, something niggling at his conscience as he'd watched the robber point his gun at the security guard.

He looked away, not wanting to watch what happened next.

Instead, his thoughts drifted.

Exactly how did Wesley's shooting tie in with Tali and those bank robberies? He couldn't think of any other reason Wesley would have been shot at Tali's bookstore unless there was a connection.

He didn't know, but he was going to make it a priority to find out.

On a whim, Mac called Cassidy—via Facetime.

Facetime was a new thing he'd begun using—his

friend Axel had insisted he should learn. Video calls were slowly growing on him.

Mac finally had to insist that Axel stop giving him advice on modern-day dating. He had no interest in learning about Snapchat or Tinder. Of course, Axel had backed off since Tali came to town. But his friend still liked to keep him updated on all the latest trends —from technology to social media.

Cassidy answered on the first ring, and her face appeared on the screen, her office in the background. "Good afternoon, Mac. I heard you had some more excitement in The Crazy Chefette today—after the near hit-and-run. I was halfway expecting to get a phone call about that confrontation with Arlo Simmons."

"If it had been up to me, I would've sent you after that guy. But Tali asked me to back off. Said Arlo was just grieving."

Cassidy's eyebrows flicked up in unspoken thought. "Tali was nicer than I would have been. But I'm assuming that's not what you're calling about."

"It's not. Any update on the driver who tried to run Tali over?"

"Actually, yes. You're not going to believe this, but the vehicle belongs to none other than Allan Warwick. However, he reported it stolen first thing this morning."

Chewy? Again?

That seemed like too much of a coincidence.

"Did you question him?"

"We did. He was at the house all morning. Three people can vouch for him."

Mac frowned. "He could have hired someone. If he was involved with those prior crimes, then he's clever and smart."

"Motive?" Cassidy asked.

Mac frowned. "That's a great question. But as far as I'm concerned, Chewy is still the best suspect."

"We're keeping a close eye on him. Don't worry."

Mac also had another question. "I'm curious. I know you found the gun used to shoot Wesley. Can you remind me exactly what type of gun that was again?"

"It was a Sig Sauer. Why?"

His heart pounded harder as he licked his lips and contemplated what he was about to say.

"What are you getting at, Mac?" Cassidy tilted her head as she studied his expression over the phone screen.

"Cassidy . . . this could be nothing, but . . . those bank robberies thirty years ago . . . the weapon used in those homicides was never found. But it was a Sig Sauer."

CHAPTER 11

Tali was back at the bookstore, standing in the center of the space, and staring at her crumbling dreams as a sense of grief lingered in the air.

Why had so much bad stuff already happened here at her little shop? She didn't want any of those memories to taint what was supposed to be a place of healing.

Opening a bookstore had been a dream of hers for so long, and now it was becoming reality. However, her reality was being marred with murder.

Would she ever be able to look at this shop and not remember the unsettling things that had happened here?

She didn't have the answer to that question.

Tali let out a deep breath.

She'd been back from breakfast for more than an hour. After checking the locks on her doors, she hadn't been able to resist doing a little research on Atlanta National. She'd grabbed her computer and pulled up a webpage featuring all the board members.

She'd studied each of their faces.

Was one of them responsible for last night's shooting?

It was hard to say.

Chewy seemed the most likely suspect.

But Arlo had a temper. However, would he really shoot his own son?

Tali found that hard to believe.

There was a new man on the board, a guy named Perry Johnson.

Tali studied his face, but he didn't look familiar.

The other board members were women. Could one of them be responsible?

Maybe. But Tali didn't think so. Call it a gut instinct.

If the person who'd shot Wesley wasn't a board member, who would it be? Was someone else from Georgia here on the island? Had this person seized the opportunity to shoot Wesley, knowing the police might assume the shooting was connected to crimes from thirty years ago?

It was a possibility.

Finally, Tali had given up on her research, knowing she needed to do something else in order to clear her head.

No sooner had she begun to straighten up some books did a face appear at her door.

Not one face but three.

Her spirits lifted when she recognized the members of her book club.

Quirky Serena Lavinia, part-time ice cream lady and part-time intrepid reporter. Quiet Cadence Garth, Lisa Dillinger's cousin who'd moved here recently to help out with Lisa's kids and the restaurant. And enigmatic and entertaining Abby Mendez, who was starting a theater group.

Tali ushered them all into the bookstore, thankful for the distraction.

"What brings you all here?" Tali asked as everyone—including Sugar—huddled around her.

That dog was part human. Some days, Tali was certain of it.

At once, questions began flying.

Tali had no doubt her friends had already heard about the near hit-and-run as well as the confrontation with Arlo at The Crazy Chefette this morning. The girls had a million questions for her—the most prominent one being if Tali was okay.

And she was.

Once those details were out of the way, they all moved to the cluster of couches and chairs where they could talk on a deeper level.

"So, the people your husband used to work for just happen to be on this island right now for a corporate retreat?" Serena raised her eyebrows as she gave Tali a knowing look.

"I know how it sounds, and I agree it's strange. But yes, that *is* the case." Tali leaned down and swooped Sugar into her arms.

"Where are they staying? It's not exactly like we have corporate retreat centers laid out all over the island." Cadence reached over to pet Sugar. "I mean, I know I haven't been here long, but that's my impression, at least. I overhear Lisa and Braden talking about things all the time."

Lisa was married to Braden, one of the police officers here on the island.

"I was told the group rented a huge house with eight bedrooms, and they're staying there. They brought in their own private chef for the event." Abby shrugged after dropping her news. "I overheard the property manager for the place talking. He stopped by the farmer's market, and I just happened to be there. Nothing is really a secret on this island. We all know that."

"Hey—the house you mentioned . . . is that the big white house down on Ocean Lane?" Serena tapped her bright red lips. "Beach Haven or something?"

"I think it is." Abby nodded enthusiastically.

"I actually know one of the women who helps clean that place." Serena stared off into space a moment as if in thought.

Tali didn't know where Serena was going with that statement. But she simply listened and tried to be patient as her friends talked this through. These ladies were good sounding boards, and their love of mysteries often offered some pretty useful knowledge in these situations.

"In fact, my friend Roberta was looking for some extra help cleaning," Serena continued. "Her company is short-staffed, and the people at this retreat apparently want them to come in every day to clean. Almost like at a hotel, you know?"

Tali had a better idea of where Serena was going with this, but she didn't want to jump to conclusions. However, Tali knew Serena well enough at this point that she dreaded what the girl might say next.

"I should offer to help." Serena shrugged with overblown innocence.

And there it was.

"Why would you do that?" Cadence beat Tali to

the question.

"Because our best suspects are staying there. Maybe one of them will say something. Or maybe I'll see something in a bedroom to indicate exactly what's going on. I mean, it can't be a coincidence they picked Lantern Beach, right? Plus, I've read *The Maid*. There could be all kinds of evidence hiding in that house."

"That's a terrible idea," Tali said with a definitive shake of her head.

"Why do you say that?" Serena stared at her as if honestly confused.

"Because we have someone with a gun loose on this island. This person didn't hesitate to pull the trigger once. He could have another weapon and do it again."

"But if I do my job well, no one will even know I'm there to snoop. They'll just think I'm cleaning." Serena said the words as if she didn't have a worry in the world.

"Serena . . ." Tali's voice held warning.

Serena shrugged in a laid-back manner. "It was just an idea. But if anything were to happen to me, you'd take care of Scoops, right?"

"Serena!" The word came out louder than Tali intended.

"I was just kidding. But Scoops and Sugar are best

friends . . ."

Tali let out a long, slow breath as she tried to control her racing thoughts. "I appreciate the fact you want to help, but if anything happened to you because of me, I wouldn't be able to forgive myself. Do you understand that?"

As Tali stroked Sugar, the dog barked in agreement.

Serena stared at Tali another moment before nodding. "Of course. You're right. I would never want to put you in that position."

Tali wanted to believe Serena's words . . . but she knew Serena well enough to know that the woman liked to take matters into her own hands.

Tali frowned and prayed that the situation wouldn't turn any worse.

———

Mac's thoughts continued to race through all the evidence.

Chewy's gun had been found after the shooting yesterday.

Chewy's car had been the one to almost run down Tali.

The man seemed like the most obvious suspect. But he claimed his gun had recently been stolen. If it had been used in those bank robberies three decades ago, why had he kept it?

What sense would that make?

Cassidy would run ballistics, and Mac was curious about the results. But he knew these things could take time.

Chewy also claimed his car had been stolen this morning—a fact that Cassidy had confirmed. He *had* called the station, and Officer Leggott had gone out to take his statement.

Was someone trying to set the man up?

That's how it appeared. But Mac wasn't ruling Chewy out as a suspect either.

As Jimmy's image flashed into his mind, Mac swallowed the lump in his throat.

Could he have been wrong about Jimmy all those years ago?

He didn't know.

It wasn't often he doubted his policing skills. But he *was* imperfect. If he'd made a mistake, he wanted to know.

For his own sake.

And for Tali's.

For the next couple of hours, Mac made more phone calls and watched more videos.

When he finished that, he made a list of everyone who was here for the corporate retreat.

Arlo Simmons, Chief Executive Officer

Wesley Simmons, Chief Operations Officer

Allan "Chewy" Warwick, Vice President

Perry Johnson, Chief Financial Officer

Deanna Robinson, Secretary

Maisie Robinson, Secretary's Assistant

Nancy Fetterman, Member at Large

Kathleen Palmer, Member at Large

Mac found each of their pictures online and studied them, trying to commit each image to memory.

On a whim, Mac called one of his former colleagues, someone who just happened to be the current police chief in Atlanta.

Glen Faulkner answered on the first ring. He was the most dedicated police officer Mac had ever met. In fact, he'd gone through three marriages, all of them ending when he chose his career over those relationships.

That fact had earned him quite the reputation.

"It's been a long time," Glen said.

"Yes, it has." Mac made small talk for only a few minutes before getting to the point. "What are the chances the Atlanta National robbers could be rein-terviewed?"

The men had received a hefty sentence for their involvement in the crimes—especially since two people had died. Mac wasn't even sure when—or if —they'd ever be eligible for parole.

"Reinterviewed?" Surprise rang through Glen's voice. "All these years later? What's going on?"

Mac gave him a quick rundown.

"That's an interesting twist." Glen grunted. "You want to talk to them yourself? You know Davis passed away about twelve years ago."

"Then the other two. I don't think I'll be able to travel to Atlanta, not with everything going on here. I was hoping you could have one of your guys talk to them and then fill me in afterward."

Glen paused, not saying anything for a moment. "What do you think this will prove?"

"It's been a long time. I wonder if any of them might change their story or be willing to open up a little more. At this point, they don't have a lot to lose. They've already spent the majority of their lives behind bars."

Glen grunted. "Let me see what I can do—but only because you're a friend."

"I appreciate it, Glen. I'll send a list of questions over."

They ended the call a few minutes later.

Mac hoped that something might come from that conversation.

Because they desperately needed answers.

CHAPTER 12

The book club ladies had stayed another hour before they each had to leave. Their departures came just in time.

Tali had invited Deanna and Maisie for dinner, but she still had to get the food ready for them.

She ran to the store and picked up everything she needed to make chicken pot pie. Deanna's husband, Rick, had always loved that dish.

Just as the oven buzzed, Tali heard a knock on the door below. She rushed downstairs, Sugar in her arms, to greet Deanna and Maisie.

Maisie, as usual, threw her arms around Tali. But Deanna greeted Tali with a stiff nod—one that Tali brushed off. She was too old for that kind of drama.

"I'm so glad you both could make it," Tali said

instead. "I know you're busy, but this means a lot to me. Come on upstairs."

Neither of the ladies had seen her apartment yet.

Once upstairs, Tali showed them around her humble abode—one that currently smelled like crusty bread, gravy, and chicken. Despite the small size, the living area had great views—of the ocean on one side and the boardwalk on the other. Tali loved watching out the windows.

As to be expected, Maisie seemed impressed and Deanna not so much. Tali knew this place didn't compare to Deanna's five thousand square foot house back in Georgia.

But she didn't care. She was happy here, and that's what mattered.

The three of them made generic chitchat about the apartment and the island before sitting down to eat. Tali lifted up a prayer before serving the food. Then she lifted up her own silent prayer that this conversation would go well.

She could use all the help she could get.

"So, what brought you to Lantern Beach of all places, Tali?" Deanna asked, that same judgmental tone to her voice.

Not even food steaming on her plate or a glistening glass of sweet tea could soften the woman's cool stiffness.

Tali had told her sister-in-law she was moving here, but Deanna hadn't had much to say about it then. That was fine. The two of them had never run their life choices past each other.

"I've vacationed here in the past," Tali said. "I always thought this island was great, the kind of area where it would be perfect to retire. So, I figured why not take that risk and come here? What did I have to lose at this point, right?"

Deanna made a face. "The nearest hospital is far away if you need it. You are getting older, you know."

Tali sucked in a deep breath and reminded herself to be patient. "I know. But wherever you live there are risks. I suppose that's a tradeoff I'm willing to make. There's something about the beach that's always seemed very healing to me."

"Well, I hope this little business can support you." Deanna didn't bother to hide her doubt. "You should have come to me. I could have done a cash flow and risk analysis. Maybe Atlanta National could have even given you a loan."

Tali swallowed her food, almost hating this small talk in light of everything that had happened. And there was no way she would have gone to Atlanta National—not after the way they'd thrown Jimmy under the bus and snubbed Tali as if she were complicit as well.

"Not to change the subject, but I can't believe Wesley is in a coma," Maisie said as she picked at her food.

This was a subject change Tali could get on board with. "Did you know him well?"

"No, not really. But we talked a few times. He seemed nice enough."

Tali wiped her mouth with a napkin. "What is he like?"

"Quiet," Deanna answered before Maisie could talk. "Doesn't have many friends. Never married. He's a smart man, but everyone knows he's only on the board because his father started the bank. He's not the most responsible employee. Someone constantly has to hold his hand and walk him through his job."

"That's how these things work sometimes." Tali paused. "Are you saying he is a recluse?"

Deanna raised her shoulders. "I don't know if I'd say that. He has a couple of friends he likes to hang out with, I guess. I don't exactly ask him personal questions. It wouldn't be appropriate."

"How did he act after you all came here?" Tali continued.

"Nervous," Maisie quickly interjected. "He seemed nervous—more than usual. I asked him about it, and he just said he had a lot on his mind."

Tali wanted to ask more about the corporate retreat but, before she could, Deanna jumped in with a question of her own.

"That man who insisted on looking at my phone last night . . . I think you called him Mac." Deanna took another bite of her food, not offering any praise or criticism.

"That's right. Mac MacArthur. He's the island's mayor." Tali took a piece of her crust and sneaked it to Sugar, who gobbled it down and waited at her feet as if hoping for more.

"He looked familiar . . ." Deanna stated.

Dread pooled in Tali's stomach as she realized where this conversation was going.

She cleared her throat before saying, "He actually used to live in Atlanta. I didn't know him back then. In fact, the two of us didn't realize our past connection until after I moved here and we got to know each other a little bit."

Deanna narrowed her eyes thoughtfully—or maybe judgmentally. "The two of you seem as if you're good friends."

"Mac has really been there for me since I arrived here. That's true."

"What did he do back in Atlanta?" She tilted her head as she listened, carefully soaking in every detail.

Deanna wasn't going to drop this . . .

And here it went.

Tali wiped her mouth again, her appetite suddenly gone, before she said, "He was a police officer."

Deanna's eyes lit with realization. "Wait . . . he's one of the men who put Jimmy behind bars, isn't he?"

"He was only doing his job." Tali couldn't believe she was defending Mac for arresting her husband. Yet here she was.

Deanna jumped to her feet, fire lighting in her eyes.

Even Sugar startled and rose to his feet to regard Deanna.

"How can you even associate with a man who ruined Jimmy's life?" Deanna screeched. "He nearly ruined my life and Rick's life as well. Rick got Jimmy that job at the bank. How do you think it looked for him when his brother was arrested?"

A fire seemed to ignite inside Tali as well. "How can *you* even work for a man who may have set Jimmy up?"

"What? You think Arlo set Jimmy up? That's preposterous." Deanna turned her nose up at the thought.

The only people who used words like *preposterous* were people who were *preposterously* snobby. Tali had always believed that, and she stood behind it now.

"I'm just saying that things aren't always as simple as you might think." Tali forced herself to remain calm.

"I can't even sit here and have dinner with you knowing what I know now." Deanna threw her napkin on her chair and then turned to Maisie. "We need to leave. Now."

"But Mom . . ." Maisie frowned. "I'd really like to catch up with Aunt Tali. Please. I've missed her."

Betrayal stretched through Deanna's gaze. "Fine. But I'm leaving."

"Deanna . . ." Tali muttered.

But her sister-in-law wanted nothing to do with her.

As Deanna stormed away, Tali let her go.

————

Still at his desk, Mac studied pictures of Wesley Simmons he'd pulled from the man's social media.

The photos went way back.

Even though Facebook hadn't been around thirty years ago, some older photos had been scanned and uploaded to his page.

The man didn't appear adventurous. Most of the snapshots of him were taken in the office or in homes —not exotic locations or picturesque mountain hikes. He had a weak smile, and his gaze appeared rather lifeless.

As Mac studied the photos, he realized the man didn't exactly seem threatening. In fact, Wesley looked lost—even more so as he grew older.

It was hard to believe the man was now in the hospital fighting for his life.

However, studying Wesley's social media appeared to be getting him nowhere.

Finally, Mac stood. He needed to stretch his legs. Besides, walking always helped him clear his head.

His earlier conversation with Tali hadn't gone the way he wanted. He wasn't sure they'd ever get over this hurdle between them.

Unless he could convince her that Jimmy had deserved to be behind bars.

But Mac wasn't sure that would ever happen. Besides, *was* that what he really wanted? To taint the image she had of her husband?

He frowned as he stepped outside. There didn't seem to be a way to win in this situation.

Before he even left the parking lot, he spotted someone walking toward him.

Axel.

The man was tall with messy dark hair and mischievous eyes. He'd been quite the womanizer until Olivia Rollins had captured his heart.

Mac expected a proposal any time now.

Mac and Axel liked to give each other a hard time. But Axel was also extremely smart and capable —a good sounding board.

"I had a moment, so I thought I'd check on you." Axel paused in front of him and leaned against the brick wall as if he had all the time in the world. He nodded at Mac's head. "How's your injury?"

Mac touched the spot where he'd been hit. "I can't complain."

"Did you figure out who shot that man?" Axel crossed his arms as he waited for Mac's answer.

"No, but I suspect it's someone who came with Wesley here on the retreat. They make the most sense." He glanced at Axel. "What's your take on it, Frogman?"

He could tell by Axel's tone that he'd been thinking about it.

Axel let out a breath. "The gunman is most likely still on the island if he's the one who tried to run Tali over this morning. He won't leave until he's success- ful, right? The fact Tali was targeted means that someone feels threatened by her."

"But why?"

"That's the question. Does this person fear Wesley told Tali something before he was shot? Does he fear Tali will figure everything out?"

"My best guess is that the shooter is also the fourth gunman," Mac said. "He's gotten away with this crime for thirty years. He doesn't want to go to prison now."

"Of course not. So he's going to do whatever it takes not to do that—including silencing anyone who threatens him."

As Axel's statement hung in the air, someone across the street caught Mac's eye.

A man Mac had never seen before started walking toward the town hall building but froze.

He stared at Mac and Axel.

Took a step back.

Then he started to run.

"Hey, wait!" Mac shouted.

He and Axel took off after the guy.

But as the man reached the street corner and darted across, a car zoomed down the street.

The vehicle plowed into the man, and he flew into the air.

Mac and Axel paused in horror as they watched the man's limp body hit the ground.

CHAPTER 13

"'m so sorry that you're in the middle of this," Tali told Maisie after Deanna stormed out.

The two of them remained at the dining room table, not touching their food. Instead, they both almost seemed dazed.

"It's okay. As I'm sure you know, my mom isn't always the easiest person to get along with." Maisie frowned and took another sip of her sweet tea.

Tali didn't say anything. The polite side of her didn't want to verbally agree with Maisie, even though the words were true.

"It hasn't been *that* long since we've spoken. I didn't realize you were also working for the bank now." Tali settled back in her chair, wishing she could relax. But she had too much on her mind to do that.

Maisie shrugged. "The paper company I was working for downsized. It was all very sudden, and I'd just bought that new house. I couldn't afford not to make my payments. That's when my mom said there was a new position opening up at the bank. She needed an assistant, and she wanted to give me the job."

Tali couldn't imagine working for Deanna, but again she said nothing in an effort to not cause more problems. However, Deanna was the type who got what she wanted. She'd never thought the paper company paid Maisie enough, and Tali had to wonder if Deanna had jumped on the opportunity to have her daughter work for her.

"I'm surprised you were able to come on the corporate retreat," Tali said instead. "I thought it was only for board members."

"Mom asked me if I would come under the stipulation that we'd share a room. Of course, most people can't bring their assistants because they can't share rooms, so the situation was a little different with Mom and me."

Tali shifted in her chair, rubbing her foot against Sugar's head as she did. "I'm not trying to be nosy, but your mom doesn't seem like the type to ask someone to come with her on her corporate retreat. She's pretty independent."

Maisie lowered her gaze. "Between you and me, doctors are doing some testing on her now. It could be Parkinson's. I'm not supposed to know, but I accidentally saw an email from her doctor's office."

Despite Tali's hard feelings toward the woman, her heart softened. She wouldn't wish Parkinson's on anyone.

"I'm so sorry to hear that, sweetie." She patted her niece's hand sympathetically.

Maisie shrugged, looking as if she were holding back emotions. "Me too. She's had some tremors in her hands and some balance issues—again, she didn't tell me. I just observed them. But I'm trying not to worry until she knows something for sure. I personally think it's the stress she's been under that's causing her episodes."

"She's been under a lot of stress lately?" Tali wanted to believe she was asking that question entirely because she really wanted to know and was concerned about her sister-in-law. But she was also curious about what was going on at the bank.

"You know Arlo isn't easy to work with." Maisie raised her eyebrows and offered a knowing look. "I've seen that firsthand. His coffee has to be a certain temperature, or you'll get an earful. He'll fire someone for looking at him the wrong way. And if he's in one of his moods, you just need to stay out of his way."

Tali offered a half eye roll before nodding. "That's what your Uncle Jimmy always said."

"Anyway, I think Mom should just retire. But she says she's not ready."

Tali shifted in her seat, her mind still racing over everything she'd learned.

Things weren't always as they appeared on the surface, were they?

Not even when it came to her sister-in-law.

———

As the paramedics helped the man, Mac and Axel remained close. Officer Dillinger tried to calm down the driver, a woman in her early thirties, as hysteria gripped her. She cried, threw her arms in the air, and then buried her face in her hands.

The man had run right out in front of her. There wasn't anything she could have done to avoid him. But still, the event had been traumatic for her.

"I've seen that man before," Axel said as he stared at the scene.

Mac turned toward him. "You have?"

"When I went to the bookshop for the grand opening, he was walking outside. I mean, a lot of people were."

Mac had gotten a good look at the man, but he didn't seem familiar. He was probably in his thirties, with dark-blond hair and a slim build. The man was clean-cut—more of a businessman than the blue-collar worker type.

"Do you think he's associated with the retreat?" Axel asked.

Mac shook his head. "Not that I know of. I've studied everyone on the retreat, and he wasn't one of them."

"Then why did he run when he saw us?"

"That's an excellent question. He definitely looked spooked."

Mac's jaw tightened. He didn't like this. Not at all.

He patiently waited until Cassidy made her way over to them, a look of exhaustion on her face.

"Here we are again," she started.

"Yes, we are," Mac said. "Anything you can tell us? How's that man doing?"

"He hit his face when he landed, so he's having trouble speaking. We're taking him to the clinic to be checked out."

"Do you know who he is?" Axel asked.

"His name is Aidan Parker, and he's from . . . Georgia."

Alarm raced through Mac.

Maybe this guy *was* somehow connected.

He needed to speak to Tali. See if she recognized that name.

Maybe this was the guy they were looking for.

CHAPTER 14

Tali and Maisie chatted quite a bit longer. They'd talked about Maisie's love life for a while, but she said she was still single and looking. Said a few guys had shown interest, but none whom she liked.

Maisie was gorgeous, so Tali had no doubt her niece had a whole lineup of men who'd love her attention.

She had mentioned one man in particular who'd asked her out several times over the past few months. She'd told him no each time. Part of the reason Maisie had come on this trip with her mom was to get away from him. He'd been too persistent for her comfort.

Tali didn't like the sound of that and was glad Maisie was here.

But Tali also had some other pressing questions—questions she hoped Maisie might want to answer for her.

They were onto dessert and coffee when she asked the first.

"Who's here from the company this week?" Tali sipped her coffee, trying not to look overly eager.

"Arlo, Chewy, my mother, me . . . and I'm not sure you'd know the rest of the board. They're fairly new."

"In full disclosure, I looked up their information online earlier today." Tali shrugged. "I was curious. What about the new guy? Perry?"

From his photo, Tali noted the bank's chief financial officer looked close to sixty with thick dark hair, a wide smile, and friendly eyes.

"Perry?" Maisie let out a breath. "He just started at the bank last year. I don't know what else to say about him except maybe that he's a talker, and he drives my mom crazy. I don't really know that much about him. But I think he'd just moved to Atlanta from Florida, so he doesn't have a strong connection to the area yet."

Tali was undeterred. "What's the overall atmosphere in the beach house?"

Maisie let out a long breath, blowing her bangs out of her face. "Honestly? There's a lot of tension right now. A lot of whispering. Even some anger—mostly from Arlo."

"I still can't believe he doesn't want to be with Wesley in the hospital." Tali frowned. "That has us all a little stumped."

"You're not the only one. I do know that Arlo and his ex-wife have a very contentious relationship. I'm not sure it would be good for Wesley to have them both arguing while he's fighting for his life. Plus, I heard Arlo say something like there was nothing he could do for Wesley in his son's current state. But that, as soon as Wesley woke up, he'd head out to the hospital to see him."

"I understand." Tali shifted again. "I hope I don't sound too intrusive by asking this, but there were eight people here on this retreat, right?"

Maisie nodded, her eyes widening with an eagerness to help. "That's right."

"I know you and your mom were here at my shop when the shooting occurred. Wesley was the one shot. That leaves three people accounted for, but what about the other five? Where were they last night?"

"You're trying to see who doesn't have an alibi, aren't you?" Curiosity sparked in her gaze—curiosity that quickly turned to fear as she continued. "Wait . .

. you think someone from the corporate retreat could be responsible?"

Tali swallowed hard as she tried to choose her words wisely.

———

After a moment of contemplating what to say, Tali licked her lips.

She tried to keep her voice calm so she wouldn't upset her niece. "It only makes sense that someone from the retreat might be the one behind the attempted homicide. It clearly wasn't a random crime."

Maisie's eyes remained wide and frightened. "You're right. However . . . Arlo, Chewy, and Perry were on a nighttime fishing trip. The two other ladies who are with us had massages scheduled for those hours. So, everyone at the house has an alibi."

Disappointment bit at Tali. But she still had more questions. "Why didn't Wesley go fishing with the other guys?"

"I heard him remind his dad he didn't like fishing."

"Was it offshore?"

Maisie shook her head. "No, they were surf fishing on the beach."

"So, any of those guys could have stepped away for a few minutes . . . maybe for long enough to shoot Wesley."

Maisie cringed as if uncomfortable with the question. "I . . . I suppose."

Tali let that revelation sink in.

Chewy and Arlo were still her top suspects—especially if one of them had been able to slip away from surf fishing. After all, Wesley's shooting and the subsequent escape had probably only taken thirty minutes.

However, she still had a hard time believing Arlo would shoot his own son.

Hopefully, Cassidy had talked to everyone on the fishing excursion and was collecting more evidence even as they spoke.

She didn't know this Perry guy who was on the board, but he hadn't been around during the original shootings, which made him seem a less likely suspect.

"There's one other thing you should know . . ." Maisie said. "I think everyone is going home tomorrow. No one is really having fun anymore. So . . . if your suspect is a part of our retreat, you don't have much time to figure it out."

As Maisie's statement lingered in her mind, Sugar let out a low growl.

"What is it, boy?" Tali muttered.

Sugar barked, his ears perked.

Tali shushed him and listened.

Was that a noise downstairs?

She stiffened.

Maybe someone had knocked on the door.

Sometimes it was hard to hear from up here.

Tali excused herself to go find out.

But tension filled her when she walked down the stairs.

Who could be here now?

And did she really want to know?

CHAPTER 15

Tali reached the bottom of the stairs and glanced around.

The exterior door had glass at the top, which allowed her to see outside. When she didn't see anyone standing there, her suspicions instantly rose.

Footsteps sounded behind her, and she swirled around. She let out a breath as she realized it was Maisie.

Of course.

Tali should've known, but after everything that had happened, she was just so jumpy.

"Everything okay?" Maisie held Sugar as she stood halfway down the stairs.

"It's probably fine. It's just that I heard something down here . . . a knock."

"I heard it too."

Tali stared at the door again, wondering if someone was hiding on the other side, out of sight. Maybe she couldn't see them in the darkness.

But if that was the case, they would knock again, right?

Hesitantly, Tali took a few steps toward the door and paused.

There was no more knocking.

Instead, she paced farther into the bookstore.

Maybe she could peek out the picture window there.

Maisie followed her, her eyes wide and her shoulders stiff. "I don't see anyone."

"It could have come from next door. Sometimes I can hear things going on over at the surf shop."

"That was probably it." Maisie looked—and sounded—unconvinced as she said the words.

Just as Tali turned to head back upstairs, she heard another noise.

So did Sugar. The dog began barking.

Was someone on the island up to some Halloween mischief?

Tali froze as her muscles tightened.

As she glanced at the bookshelf in the center of the room, she saw a movement between the books.

Sugar barked louder.

Fear raced down Tali's spine.

Maisie scooted closer to Tali, and they took a step toward the bookcase.

Had her neighbor's black cat slipped inside the shop again? It had already happened twice, and Tali was afraid the feline was going to wreak havoc. Plus, Sugar didn't like the cat.

If the animal had gotten inside, Tali needed to find him.

But before she could search, the bookcase suddenly tilted.

Then it crashed toward Tali, Maisie, and Sugar.

———

Mac walked up to the bookstore, ready to give Tali an update and check on her.

But just as he reached it, he glanced through the window, and his lungs froze.

A demented man—no, a *Dementor*—lingered in the shadows inside.

The next instant, the bookshelf began toppling toward Tali and her niece. The Dementor sprinted toward the back of the store.

Wasting no time, Mac tried to open the door.

But it was locked.

Instead, he rammed his shoulder into it.

The wood facing splintered, but the door opened.

He raced toward the two ladies.

Maisie had raised her arms and stopped the bookshelf midair before it collided with Tali. Books had fallen, and the ladies would probably have some bruises.

But the whole situation could've turned out much worse.

Moving quickly, Mac took the shelf from Maisie and pushed it upright.

He frowned. He'd been here when that bookshelf had been installed. Safety brackets had been mounted on the floor to ensure nothing like this would happen.

A bad feeling brewed in his gut.

Mac gave a quick glance at Maisie. The young woman appeared shaken but not visibly injured.

"Good job catching this," he muttered.

Then he went to Tali and knelt on the floor beside her. She hadn't fallen hard, but the cascading books had knocked her off her feet. Plus, she was already bruised from the earlier incident at The Crazy Chefette.

"Are you okay?" He studied Tali's face.

She looked dazed and . . . maybe even a touch angry.

But she nodded. "I . . . I think so."

She glanced down at Sugar beneath her. Of course, Tali had sheltered her dog from any falling debris. The Westie hopped from her arms, took a few steps, and gave himself a good shake.

Mac rose to his feet again and helped Tali up.

Tali turned toward him, her gaze locking on his. "Go get that guy. He was just here—he can't be far away."

He thought she'd never ask.

Wasting no more time, Mac hurried toward the back door.

CHAPTER 16

Mac felt like this was a replay from last night.

As he stepped out the back door of Tali's place and looked around, he saw no one.

Probably five minutes had passed since the man had been inside. There was a chance this guy could've gotten away.

But not *that* far away.

He headed left toward the rest of the shops.

As he did, he scanned everything around him—both to the sides and above him.

But he saw no one.

Not even a cat jumped out in front of him this time.

Mac searched for two blocks.

But whoever had been out here was now gone.

He glanced at the apartments located overtop some of the shops.

Some of them were rentals.

Realization washed through him.

What if this guy was staying somewhere close?

That could explain how the man had been able to escape so quickly.

Mac frowned.

That was definitely something he needed to look into—but he wasn't going to be able to do it alone.

Plus, how did Aidan Parker tie into all of this?

———

In what was seemingly becoming a routine, Tali gave Cassidy her statement . . . again.

Maisie held Sugar in the corner of the bookstore and waited to be questioned, a frown on her face.

The poor girl . . . she shouldn't have to experience all this. It was too much—for anyone, really.

In the middle of their conversation, Mac returned.

Tali knew by the frown on his face that he hadn't caught the man.

"Whoever was behind this was clever." Mac crossed his arms and scowled as he paused beside Tali and Cassidy. "He had an escape plan."

Cassidy glanced at Tali. "I assure you that we're

working hard to get to the bottom of this. I'm glad that neither of you were hurt any more than you were."

"Thank you."

Cassidy shifted. "Does the name Aidan Parker ring any bells with you?"

"Aidan?" Maisie said from across the room. She paced toward them, a concerned expression on her face. "I know Aidan."

Tali frowned, not sure what was going on here.

"Were you aware he was on the island?" Cassidy asked.

"What?" Maisie's voice sounded breathless. "No . . . why would he be here?"

"I'm sorry—who's Aidan?" Tali asked.

"He's that guy who asked me out, the one who was giving me the creeps."

"He followed you here?" Tali felt herself tense as she asked the question.

"I don't know." Maisie rubbed Sugar's head more vigorously. "That's what it sounds like."

"He was hit by a vehicle near the town hall," Cassidy explained. "The whole thing was a total accident. This guy saw Mac and took off in a run, darting right in front of the driver."

"Is Aidan okay?" Maisie asked.

Cassidy nodded. "He will be. But his face is

pretty busted up. He isn't able to answer many questions right now."

Maisie gasped, and her hand flew over her mouth. "Oh my goodness! Aidan likes Harry Potter. I totally forgot about that! He told me he'd love to take me down to Universal Studios so I could see The Wizarding World of Harry Potter one day. I thought it was a little weird. But . . ."

"I'd say he might be the one behind this . . . but if he was in the clinic then he obviously couldn't have been here to push down our bookshelf," Tali muttered.

"My thoughts exactly." Cassidy frowned. "This is just getting weirder and weirder. There is one other thing. Wesley got that threatening text that lured him outside. We checked Aidan's phone, and he was getting texts from that same number. Someone was clearly threatening both of them."

Tali's stomach clenched.

They needed to figure out who.

CHAPTER 17

Tali sighed, more confused than ever. "Okay, so we need to figure out why Aidan was here. But Aidan clearly wasn't the one who pushed this bookcase over. How did this guy even get inside?"

"He must have picked the lock." Cassidy moved closer. "Can you pull up the footage on your security camera?"

Tali did—but it was just as she expected.

The man was wearing that stupid Dementor costume again—and no one around had even batted an eyelash since Halloween was right around the corner.

Really—what good were these cameras if people kept learning how to work around them? The devices were supposed to bring her comfort, but they didn't.

"What was he even doing in here?" Tali glanced around as if looking for any surprises he might have left.

They all shook their heads and then looked the place over. Other than the bookshelf being emptied, nothing seemed awry.

Mac crossed the room and glanced at something on the floor before letting out a grunt.

"What is it?" Tali appeared beside him.

He pointed to the floor where three small holes were. "The shelves were bolted down. They had to be in order to pass the building inspection. Someone loosened the bolts."

Tali's hand covered her mouth as she shook her head. "So, whether we came downstairs or not, this person was planning on creating some chaos. But why? Why come back and risk being caught?"

Mac frowned again. "That's a good question."

"One more thing I thought I should mention," Cassidy said. "I just got ballistics back. The gun used to shoot Wesley and the gun used in the robberies are one and the same."

———

Tali continued to process everything that had happened as the minutes rolled past.

Finally, she turned back to Cassidy, knowing she needed to do something to occupy her thoughts. "I hate seeing my bookstore like this. Can I start cleaning up?"

"Dillinger already looked through everything and didn't find any evidence. So feel free. But if you find anything out of place, please let us know."

Twenty minutes later, Cassidy was gone, the bookshelf was reattached to the floor, and Mac, Maisie, and Tali were picking up the books. Tali would need to go through each of them, organize them by genre, and put them back in alphabetical order.

Of course, this guy had messed with her favorite bookshelf—the one housing her mystery and suspense novels.

Tali was too particular to *not* reorganize the books.

So, for now, she was just asking everyone to put them in stacks that she'd go through later. Some of the covers had been bent—a fact that bugged her almost as much as dog-eared book pages.

"What's this?" Maisie held up something that had partially fallen out of a book.

Why had there been a piece of paper in one of her books? Tali had bought them all brand new and placed them on the shelf right out of the box.

Tali took the folded paper from her niece and opened it.

Her heart skipped several beats as she read what was inside.

"Tali?" Mac looked at her with curiosity.

"It says, 'I know things. We need to meet.'"

"What?" Mac's shoulders rolled back as his gaze darkened. "Did anyone sign their name?"

"Yes. It's signed Wesley. And he left his phone number."

———

Mac stared at the note, which had now been placed in a bag just in case any additional prints were on it.

"Maybe Wesley came here to give you this note, Tali." Mac began pacing. "The question is: how did it end up in this book? Why didn't he just give it to you? Or have a face-to-face conversation with you?"

"Wesley is the nervous type," Maisie said as she sat in a chair, concerned wrinkles around her eyes. "He really seems to want to please his father. But that's an impossible task. One time, he said something to me about how he wanted to be free. I didn't know exactly what that meant."

"So, he came here wanting to talk to Tali about something—possibly the whole bank robbery thing.

Maybe he was going to slip Tali this note as a way of initiating the conversation." Mac stared in the distance as he put together his thoughts. "He left you his phone number so you could call him to set up a meeting?"

Tali rubbed her arms, a trepid expression on her face. "I guess so. Maybe he didn't feel comfortable enough writing down whatever it was he wanted to talk to me about. What could that even be?"

Mac's gaze latched onto hers. "Did you know Wesley back when Jimmy worked for the bank?"

"Not very well, but I remember seeing him at some company parties."

"What if Wesley saw something all those years ago—something that's been haunting him ever since?" Mac suggested. "Add with that, Wesley was the one who picked this location. Maybe he chose it because he knew you were here. Maybe once he arrived, he heard about your event and knew it would be a good opportunity to have a personal conversation with you. But he was also nervous, and that's why he wrote this note."

"And he left it in a book?" Maisie pulled Sugar closer. "That's what doesn't make sense to me. How was Aunt Tali supposed to find it?"

"Wait . . . this was in *Misery* . . ." Tali muttered.

"What about it?" Mac asked.

"Someone texted me during the party to ask if I had a copy. With everything that happened, I all but forgot about it."

"So you think Wesley left that note there and then texted you, knowing you'd probably see the paper he'd left for you when you grabbed the book?" Maisie asked.

"I think so." Tali shook her head, probably mentally fussing at herself for not checking earlier.

Just then the door rattled.

They all turned toward the sound and braced themselves for whatever might happen next.

CHAPTER 18

Tali held her breath, preparing herself for more trouble.

Instead, Serena stepped inside, a bright smile on her face.

"It looks like I missed something." She glanced around the shop, not bothering to hide her curiosity.

Tali released the air from her lungs and sighed. "Serena . . . we had another break-in."

Serena's eyes widened as she stepped closer to the group. "What in the world is going on? Someone is *clearly* feeling threatened."

That was it, wasn't it? If the real killer—who was possibly the fourth robber—knew that the truth might come out, then this person felt vulnerable. Now he wanted to silence anyone who knew what really happened—before he could be exposed.

The thought sent a chill through Tali.

Then she noticed what Serena was wearing.

Khakis with a white shirt and a name tag . . . a name tag that read Coastal Cleaners.

"Serena . . ." Tali's voice held a motherly warning.

Serena glanced at her name tag and shrugged, unaffected by Tali's tone.

Mac stepped closer and crossed his arms. "What did you do?"

She shrugged again. "I volunteered to help my friend with housecleaning at Beach Haven."

"You did *what*?" Mac's sharp words reflected Tali's thoughts.

"It was all safe and on the up and up." Serena's gaze met Maisie's. "I mean, you're not going to tell anyone, are you?"

"I'll do whatever Aunt Tali says," Maisie said. "I'm definitely not going to do anything to put you in danger, especially now when someone's going all Dementor-like crazy around here."

Tali raised a finger in the air before saying matter-of-factly, "For the record, I told Serena that this was a very bad idea and that she shouldn't do it."

"But you're going to be glad that I did." Serena grinned.

"Why is that?" Tali asked.

"Because you'll never believe what I found."

Mac held his breath as he waited to hear what Serena had to say. The girl had a knack for getting herself in trouble. But she also had a knack for solving crimes. The trade-off left him on edge.

"When I took some trash to the can outside, I happened to glance inside the container," Serena started, light dancing in her gaze.

"And?" Tali sounded unusually impatient as she asked the question.

"There was something black inside. I almost ignored it—thought it was a black trash bag. But then I got curious—of course."

Mac wasn't sure if Serena was onto something or not, but he continued to listen, hoping for the best. "And then?"

"I used a gloved hand to pick it up." She reached into the oversized bag on her shoulder. "And this is what I found."

It was a . . . Dementor costume.

Mac's heart pounded harder. This *could* turn very interesting.

"I had to stuff it into my shirt because I heard someone coming," Serena continued. "Turned out to be Arlo and Chewy. They were arguing about something."

"Did you hear what they were saying?" Tali asked.

"They were talking about Wesley—wondering how to protect the company against bad PR. Funny . . . I would think they'd be more concerned about his well-being. Instead, they sounded annoyed with him."

Mac let that sink in. Did that make them guilty?

No.

Did it make them less than honorable people?

Absolutely.

But all those thoughts were forgotten when he looked over and saw Tali.

Her cheeks were flushed and gone was the laid-back, fun-loving woman he'd come to know.

And in her place was someone determined . . . and maybe even irate.

CHAPTER 19

Something else was bugging Mac, but he wasn't sure what.

Aidan Parker was just one piece of the puzzle here.

Someone else had been in the shop earlier—someone who may not have known that Aidan had been hit by a car. Someone who'd wanted to use Aidan as a scapegoat by placing him here on the island at just the wrong time.

Was that the truth of the matter? Or had Aidan been stalking Maisie and followed her here? Was the timing coincidental?

He found that hard to believe.

What was he missing?

"Mac?"

He snapped from his thoughts at the sound of

Tali's sweet voice. "Something is bugging me, and I'm trying to put my finger on what."

She said nothing, only studied him with understanding on her face.

But he still saw that anger brewing in her gaze.

Something that had been said earlier had angered her—maybe the fact that Arlo and Chewy only seemed concerned about their money and reputation.

They'd always been that way.

How far would they go to secure both of those assets?

As far as murder? Would they let innocent people go to prison?

It was within the realm of possibility.

And he would bet Tali shared those same thoughts.

After a few moments, Tali squared her shoulders. "Arlo and his cronies are ruthless. Selfish. They feel untouchable."

"That's all true." Mac's gaze remained on her as he wondered where she was going with that thought.

Part of him didn't want to know.

But something was clearly brewing in her mind.

Tali's thoughts continued to race, even after Cassidy left with the costume.

She turned to Mac, Serena, and Maisie, and jammed her fisted hands on her hips before announcing, "I'm going to the rental house to talk to Arlo and Chewy."

Mac's eyebrows shot up as his gaze filled with alarm. "That's not a good idea."

"I should have confronted them years ago about how they treated Jimmy. *Years ago.* I've been beating myself up ever since then because I didn't. No more —especially not when they've practically handed me the opportunity."

She stepped toward the door when Mac grabbed her arm.

"Tali . . ." he murmured. "You really need to think this through."

"There's nothing else to think through." Tali turned to him with fire blazing in her gaze. "I feel certain one of those board members knows more than they're letting on. That one of them set Jimmy up."

Mac stared at her another moment before he nodded. "I can tell you're gonna do this—with or without me. So, do it with me, okay? Let me go with you."

She considered his request before nodding. "Okay. But I'm going now."

Serena stepped forward. "I can go too—"

"No!" Tali and Mac said at the same time.

Tali rolled her shoulders back as if realizing how harsh she had sounded. "I need you to stay here, Serena. You too, Maisie. You can both hold down the fort. I can't let anything happen to you."

"But you're going to let something happen to yourself?" Maisie stared at Tali, looking a touch horrified at the thought.

Tali lowered her voice. "Nothing will happen to me. I'll have Mac with me."

But Maisie and Serena still looked unconvinced.

Everyone in the shop knew just how dicey the situation could turn.

But no one was going to talk Tali out of doing this.

All the people she loathed the most were here on Lantern Beach right now. Most likely, in the same house.

Now it was time for Tali to do what she should have done so long ago.

CHAPTER 20

Mac had a bad feeling about this. A really bad feeling.

He'd offered to drive Tali to her impromptu meeting. It was the least he could do. He'd already tried numerous approaches to convince her to change her mind.

None had worked.

As he drove toward Beach Haven, his phone rang.

It was Glen.

"I need to take this," Mac told Tali.

"Of course. Go right ahead."

He answered on his Bluetooth speaker. "Hey, Glen. I'm in the middle of something right now. But I assume if you're calling it's because you have a good reason."

"I'd like to think so. I was able to talk to two of those Atlanta National robbers myself. I just finished up with the second guy, and I thought you'd like to know what he said."

Mac glanced at Tali, trying to gauge her expression.

She stared at Mac, totally immersed in the conversation.

"I would love to know what he said," Mac said. "In full disclosure, Tali Robinson—Jimmy's wife—is here with me now. Are you okay with her listening?"

"That's fine," Glen said. "Robbie didn't actually offer any names, but he said the guy who was in charge was a great manipulator. This fourth robber promised that if anyone ever shared his identity, he'd make sure their loved ones died in a slow, painful manner. Those guys were scared. They believed him."

Mac frowned. "Whoever the man is, he didn't hesitate to pull the trigger during those robberies. He probably is a scary guy."

"I agree," Glen said. "Maybe even someone who's hiding in plain sight. Maybe even someone who's successful. That's where the manipulator part comes in. Anyway, I'm going to keep talking to them, see if either of them will crack."

"Thanks again."

"There is one more thing," Glen said. "Robbie said something that caught me by surprise. I think it just slipped out, actually."

"What's that?"

"He made it sound like their connection with the bank wasn't just feeding them information . . . but this person was the puppet master behind it all."

Mac thanked him and ended the call.

That was certainly interesting.

Just then, Mac pulled into the driveway of Beach Haven, noting the four other cars there. Most likely, everyone Tali wanted to speak with was here.

Mac wasn't sure if that was a good or a bad thing.

But they were about to find out.

———

Tali feared her adrenaline might wear off or that she'd second-guess herself. But that hadn't happened yet. No longer was she going to hide behind books and research or being polite and well-mannered.

This was a time to be bold. She had nothing to lose at this point.

In fact, she had *everything* to gain.

Especially since she thought she knew who was now behind this.

That conversation between Mac and Glen had given her the final clue she needed.

With Mac beside her, she charged toward the front door and pounded on it.

A moment later, Arlo answered. His gaze darkened when he saw Tali.

"What are you doing here?" he growled with narrowed eyes. "Did you mistakenly think you'd be welcome?"

Tali ignored him, storming into the house instead. "Good evening, Arlo."

"What do you think you're doing? Did I invite you inside?"

"Did I ask?" She kept walking, Mac behind her.

She didn't stop until she reached the living room.

Everyone inside stopped what they were doing and turned to look at her.

Chewy. Deanna. Nancy. Kathleen.

Arlo trailed behind and joined the rest of the group.

The only ones missing were Wesley, Maisie, and Perry.

She knew where Wesley and Maisie were.

But where was Perry?

Deanna was the first to jump to her feet. "Tali? What are you doing here?"

Deanna probably feared Tali would embarrass her.

She would be correct.

Tali's gaze met each person in the room. "Someone in this house set Jimmy up to take the fall for those robberies. Someone in here was truly the inside man but never owned up to it. My husband went to prison for many years because of your spinelessness. I'm not leaving here until I find out who that was."

Silence stretched through the room at her statement.

But Tali meant the words.

She wasn't leaving until she finally knew what had really happened.

CHAPTER 21

Mac felt the tension in the air, and he didn't know how this would all go down.

Probably not well.

But he had to admire Tali's courage. It took a lot to put herself in this situation.

"I think you should leave," Arlo seethed.

"And I think you should start talking." Tali raised her chin defiantly. "Someone here knows more than they're letting on. Someone here was secretly calling the shots during these robberies."

"That person died behind bars." Chewy sounded exasperated as he stood near the wet bar in the corner with some type of alcohol in his glass. "We all know the fourth robber is still at large. But he's been dormant for decades now. We've all moved on."

"Someone here authorized the bonus money that was sent to Jimmy," Tali continued, undeterred. "Who had the ability to do that?"

Arlo and Chewy glanced at each other.

"Arlo and I had the authority." Chewy glanced around the room. "Deanna also, I suppose."

Silence fell around them.

No one said anything again.

As they waited, Mac's phone buzzed. He quickly read Cassidy's text.

Aidan had been given enough pain medication to allow him to talk. Apparently, he'd been blackmailed into coming here and had been given specific instructions about where to stay and what to do once he arrived.

The blackmailer had sent Aidan pictures of his sister and threatened to hurt her if he didn't comply. Aidan admitted to trying to run Tali over. But he'd claimed he wasn't the one who'd shot Wesley.

Someone else was, as Glen said, the puppet master here.

Maybe someone here in this house.

That was exactly what Tali suspected, wasn't it?

"Okay, if you're not going to talk then I will," Tali continued. "I'll tell you what I think. Wesley knew the truth about these robberies. My guess is that he overheard people talking about everything when it all went down. For all these years, that knowledge has been eating him up."

"Leave my son out of this!" Arlo snapped.

Tali continued as if she didn't hear him. "I don't know what happened that might have triggered Wesley to want to share that information with me now. But he picked Lantern Beach for the retreat because he knew I was here. Wesley wanted to use this trip as an opportunity to tell me what he knew. Maybe even to apologize. I'm not sure."

When no one said anything else, Tali continued.

"I'm thinking he was probably nervous about it. Wesley has always been smart, but a little shy, wouldn't you say? He heard about the grand opening of my shop, so he came. He wanted to chat with me, but I was surrounded by people all night. Instead, he wrote me a note, including his phone number, and he was going to pass it to me."

"Why didn't he just pass it to you?" Chewy asked, looking stupefied—or like Tali was an idiot.

Mac didn't like that look, but he restrained himself from giving the man a piece of his mind.

"He got a text from someone demanding to meet outside," Tali said. "He left me the note in a book and then texted me with the name of the novel, assuming when I grabbed the book, I'd see his note."

"If there was a killer waiting for him, why would

he simply go outside to meet with him?" Deanna asked. "It doesn't seem smart."

"I believe someone was holding things over the heads of each of the people involved to ensure no one would sell him out," Tali said. "I'm not talking small things like money or possessions—which I realize are very important to most of you. I'm talking about people's lives."

"Seems extreme," Arlo murmured with a roll of his eyes.

"This person is smart," Tali said. "Very smart. Smart enough to stay under the radar all these years. Smart enough to stay close to keep a pulse on the situation."

"What are you getting at?" Chewy demanded.

"I'm getting to that," Tali said. "The robbers who worked with this guy knew he was unhinged. They didn't doubt he really would carry through with his threats—probably threats to kill loved ones."

Murmuring spread through the room.

But no one denied what Tali was saying.

Mac knew where she was going with this. Her words made sense.

"If what you're saying is true, why did this person hang around after Wesley was shot?" Chewy set his drink down and frowned. "What sense does it make?"

"This person is nervous now," Mac spoke up. "Sometimes when people are nervous, they make mistakes. I think this person is panicking and wanting to silence anyone who poses a threat. He's gotten away with this for a long time, and he doesn't want to be caught now."

Arlo crossed his arms. "That might be right. But you're barking up the wrong tree. No one in this room is guilty."

Tali's gaze met his. "How can you be so sure?"

"Speaking of which . . ." Mac glanced around. "Where is Perry?"

"He went on a walk," Deanna said before crossing her arms and pursing her lips in a sour expression.

Suddenly, Mac stiffened.

A strange scent filled the air.

He lifted his nose, but he already knew what it was.

Smoke.

Realization hit him, and he turned to the group around him. "We need to get out of here. Now."

Deanna's eyes widened. "What's going on?"

"I think someone just set this house on fire—in an effort to silence us all."

———

Tali felt her adrenaline surge.

She was just about to make her big reveal and now there was a . . . fire?

Mac took her hand and pulled her toward the door.

As he did, flames erupted outside the house.

Screams sounded.

Tali's heart pounded harder.

"We've got to get out of here!" Mac yelled.

Everyone scrambled toward the doors.

But each exit was blocked by fire.

They were trapped inside the house.

Just like someone had planned.

"Go to the second floor and jump from the balcony!" Mac yelled. "The sand dune below will break your fall. It's not as far down as you might think!"

Everyone rushed up the stairs and into the closest bedroom facing the ocean. They threw open the balcony doors, and a breeze rushed inside.

Glancing below, Tali saw the dune there. It was like Mac said—the mound of sand and grass was tall. Landing on it would be softer than landing on dirt.

"Let's move!" Mac yelled.

Mac and Tali helped everyone around them down, refusing to jump—not until everyone else was safe.

As Arlo landed on the dune below, Mac turned to see who else was left.

No one stood there, but . . . they were missing someone.

Mac turned toward her. "We need to get you out of here."

"But . . ." She glanced behind her.

"I'll look for anyone else. You need to go. I'll be right behind you."

The flames hadn't made it upstairs yet, but it was only a matter of time.

She glanced back at the balcony.

But before she could move, someone stepped out from the bedroom.

"Not so fast," a deep voice muttered over the crackling flames.

Tali knew this escape was too easy.

Things had just turned even uglier.

CHAPTER 22

Mac looked behind him and his muscles tensed.

Perry Johnson stood there.

And Deanna stepped out behind him.

"Deanna . . ." Tali muttered.

Yet Mac didn't hear any surprise in her voice.

She'd suspected her sister-in-law was involved, hadn't she?

Mac's gaze went to the gun in Perry's hand—a gun aimed directly at them.

"I wouldn't try anything." Perry's nostrils flared as he stepped closer. "It wouldn't be smart."

Mac studied the man.

He was deranged. Mac could see it in his gaze. His evil deeds had been haunting him—or simmering inside him—for three decades now.

Tali's attention was focused on her sister-in-law.

"Deanna . . . I knew it was you," Tali muttered.

"How would you have known that?" Deanna snapped. "Did you use your little librarian brain to figure it out?"

Mac's hands fisted at his side when he heard the mockery in the woman's voice.

Tali narrowed her eyes. "As a matter of fact, Jimmy used to always call you the puppet master. Said you pulled all the strings with Rick. That you knew how to make things work to your advantage. When the Atlanta police chief used that word to describe the perpetrator, everything made sense."

Deanna let out a snort. "Aren't you brilliant?"

Actually, Tali was brilliant. She'd finally put all the pieces together, hadn't she?

"That's not to mention the fact I caught a faint whiff of your perfume in the bookstore after that shelf came down on me. That's when I realized these crimes had your fingerprints all over them. I just had my blinders on so I couldn't see the truth."

Deanna's glare deepened. "I was eavesdropping, as well as setting up a little boobytrap for you with that bookshelf. But your little dog alerted you that I was down there."

"How could you do this?" Tali continued. "Jimmy was your brother-in-law. He loved you."

"I hated to put the blame on him, but he was the easiest person to take the fall."

Remorse filled Mac.

He'd put the wrong person behind bars.

Tali had been right.

Mac's heart pounded harder.

He'd have to deal with those emotions later.

Right now, they needed to survive.

"Did Jimmy know you were behind this?" Tali asked.

Deanna shrugged. "Hard to say. I think he suspected it. But I promised him Rick and I would look after you."

Contempt filled Tali's gaze. "You're heartless. You and Perry were seeing each other all along, weren't you? You probably got him the job at the bank."

"He had great credentials." Deanna flashed a smile at him. "We met on a business trip, where we started talking about our troubles. One thing led to another, and we came up with a plan to fix everything. Back then, Perry was a graduate student studying finance. He recruited some of his friends who'd gone to college up at UGA. He knew they owed their dealers some money, so they weren't hard to convince to help."

Tali shook her head. "You plotted every part of this."

"Rick and I had a lot of debt. We made a lot of bad choices when we were younger. We were in so deep there was no way out."

"So you ruined an innocent man's life?" Disgust saturated Tali's voice. "You let two innocent people die?"

Mac nudged himself in front of Tali, his gaze still on that gun as he felt the tension rising around them.

"I did what I had to do!" Deanna said, her nostrils flaring.

"Where did Rick think you got that money?" Tali asked.

"I'm not stupid. I put most of it away in an overseas fund. I added a little to my paycheck every month . . . said I got a raise. I saved the rest to use one day when Maisie is married, and I don't have to worry about her anymore. That's when my life is really going to begin. It's taken longer than I thought."

"Stop talking!" Perry shouted, extending the gun toward them.

Tali raised her hands in the air. "Perry . . . Deanna . . . you don't want to do this."

Deanna grimaced. "I feared Wesley might try something like this. I worked hard to make a respectable life for myself. I'm not going to let anyone ruin it."

Smoke began to gather at the ceiling inside the bedroom behind them as flames engulfed the room.

Tali coughed as the smoke poured out onto the balcony.

People yelled from the beach in the distance, encouraging them to jump.

Could the others see Deanna and Perry were with them?

The two of them probably had an excuse already concocted. They probably would say they were trying to save Mac and Tali when the flames consumed them.

Again—the two were such manipulators. People might even believe them.

Were those sirens Mac heard in the distance? He hoped so.

"How could you do this to Maisie?" Tali asked, derision in her voice.

Deanna shrugged. "She has me. She'll be okay. She's a strong girl."

The house moaned around them, and Mac knew they didn't have much time to get away. But one wrong move and this guy could shoot them.

They were between the proverbial rock and hard place.

"We can't go to prison," Deanna said. "Not now. We'll never make it out."

"You're going to burn up with this house instead?" Tali stared at them in confusion.

Their logic was lacking, to say the least.

"You're right. We can't wait here on the balcony and go up in flames. We've come too far." Deanna turned back to Tali. "Sorry we have to do this, but time is running out."

Deanna nodded at Perry.

Then Perry pulled the trigger.

————

Tali saw the gun aimed at her.

Before she could comprehend what was happening, Mac threw her onto the floor.

They both landed with an *umph*.

Tali's heart pounded out of control.

Had she been hit?

She didn't think so.

She glanced at Mac and saw blood spreading across his shoulder.

The air left her lungs. "Mac!"

His face twisted with pain. "I'm okay. Go!"

Tali looked up and saw Perry and Deanna disappear over the balcony.

They'd done what they'd come to do.

Now they were trying to save themselves. No

doubt they'd concoct a story making Tali and Mac look responsible for all this.

Tali knew one thing for sure: there was no way she was leaving Mac here.

"We need to get you up." She sat up and climbed to her feet, her body groaning after her collision with the floor.

Mac flinched but stood, holding onto his shoulder.

The house moaned again.

It was going down.

Soon.

"Come on!" Tali took Mac's arm and pulled him toward the balcony railing.

A beam fell, blocking the only way back into the house.

They didn't have much time.

"We can do this," Tali told Mac.

She helped him climb the railing.

But she knew he was fading.

What if that bullet had hit more than his shoulder?

He needed help.

Now.

From below, a crowd gathered. The group yelled for them to jump.

Tali looked back and saw that flames consumed

the entire house. It was only a matter of seconds before it would reach them.

Wasting no more time, she took Mac's hand.

"We're going to do this, Mac," she murmured. "You and me. We're sticking together. Do you understand?"

He nodded, but his eyes were glazed.

The fire roared through the house, the flames getting stronger.

Then Tali jumped, pulling Mac with her as they plummeted toward the sand dune below.

CHAPTER 23

An hour later, Tali and Mac were being treated at the Lantern Beach Medical Clinic.

Tali had heard Mac was doing okay, but she hadn't seen him for herself yet.

She couldn't stop thinking about the blood on his shoulder. The pinched look on his face. The reminders of how fragile life could be.

The good news was that the rest of the board from Atlanta National was okay. They'd escaped the fire intact.

Deanna and Perry had been caught as they tried to escape and had been arrested. They'd be going away for a long time. Now that they were behind bars, Cassidy expected the other robbers from his posse to start singing like canaries, as the saying went.

Deanna had admitted to "borrowing" the gun from Chewy thirty years ago and then returning it. Deanna had borrowed it again just last week.

Beach Haven was a total loss.

But overall, things could have been so much worse.

Doc Clemson wanted to keep Tali just a while longer for observation, which was okay with her. She wasn't leaving until she checked on Mac.

As someone knocked at the door, Tali saw Maisie poke her head inside.

Dread pooled inside her. Would her niece ever forgive her?

Or had their relationship been irreparably damaged?

In one regard, Tali didn't regret going to Beach Haven tonight. She'd said a lot of things she should have said decades ago. None of Jimmy's friends—or even his brother—had stood up for him or defended him. That was a tragedy within itself.

She only wished Maisie wasn't collateral damage in all this.

Maisie paused by the foot of Tali's bed.

"I'm so sorry, sweetheart," Tali started. "So, so sorry."

"I think when she was diagnosed with Parkinson's, she realized how little time she had left. It changed something about her—for the worst."

"That can happen."

"I suspected that Mom wasn't faithful to Dad," Maisie admitted. "It appears she was seeing Perry this whole time. I still can't believe it."

"None of us can."

Maisie cleared her throat as tears filled her gaze. "I'm glad you're okay, Aunt Tali."

"Me too." Tali shifted toward her. "What about Aidan? I heard he was being blackmailed."

"He was," Maisie said. "He wasn't as crazy as I feared—at least, I don't think he was. My mom knew he'd asked me out several times. She forced him to come here and follow her directions."

"At least he should be leaving you alone for a while. Are you going to head back to Georgia?"

She shifted. "Actually . . . I was hoping you might need help in your bookstore."

Tali's eyebrows shot up. "What?"

She nodded. "I need a job, and I love it here. I love books, and I love Sugar. And I love . . . you."

Tali's heart warmed. "I like that idea. I like it a lot."

"Good. I'm glad."

"We can talk about it more later, okay?"

"Absolutely." Maisie nodded. "I know you need to rest now. It's been a long night."

"Can you keep an eye on Sugar for me?" Tali asked.

"I'd be more than happy to."

As soon as Maisie left, Tali leaned back into her bed, her thoughts still racing.

She didn't have much time to think before someone else knocked on her door.

Her heart lifted when she saw Mac standing there.

He stepped forward, his shoulder wrapped in a bandage and a sling on his arm.

"You're okay?" she rushed as she sat up straighter.

He paused beside her bed. "I'm doing just fine."

Tali remembered how he'd thrown her out of the way of the bullet.

Remembered how he'd been willing to sacrifice himself for her.

Men like Mac didn't come around very often, and she was so thankful he'd come into her life. She'd let the past separate them for far too long.

"I was wrong." Mac's voice dropped with remorse. "I can't tell you how sorry I am, Tali. I truly am."

"You were just following the evidence," Tali said. "Deanna set Jimmy up."

Mac frowned. "She was really good at covering stuff up, wasn't she? I just can't believe I didn't see it."

"Jimmy did share some information he shouldn't have. I'm sure he didn't know what he was doing. Maybe that's why I thought I saw a touch of guilt in his gaze—that and because he knew he was a suspect and he never told me. That's part of the reason I was so blindsided."

More thoughts brewed in her mind.

Finally, she cleared her throat and said, "I also have to wonder if Jimmy suspected Deanna might be involved. But he was so loyal. I wonder if he kept his mouth shut and took the fall for her rather than ruining his brother's life?"

"I can't tell you that . . ." Mac squeezed her hand. "I don't feel like I can say I'm sorry enough."

"You saved my life tonight." Tali grasped his hand. "You took a bullet for me. I'd say you've more than made up for it."

"I don't know about that . . ."

"I'm hoping you'll let me give you a proper thank you sometime."

He raised his eyebrows. "You know you don't have to do that . . . but I *am* intrigued."

She grinned. "As soon as we're out of here, I've got some planning to do."

CHAPTER 24

Two days later, Lantern Beach's annual costume contest and fall festival filled the boardwalk with children dressed as superheroes and princesses, entirely too much candy, and sounds of local musician Carter Denver singing "Monster Mash."

Pumpkin carving contests took place near the Ferris wheel, a chili cookoff was happening by The Crazy Chefette, and a beach hayride delighted people of all ages.

So much had happened since Perry and Deanna's arrests.

Wesley had awoken from his coma and confirmed their theories were correct. He'd overheard a conversation between Deanna and someone else while at a company party. He knew she was involved but had been too timid to come forward.

He'd felt guilty about it all these years and had purposefully chosen Lantern Beach so he could talk to Tali face-to-face. Jimmy had always been kind to Wesley, and Wesley had felt awful knowing Jimmy had wrongfully been placed behind bars.

Deanna, however, had caught wind of what Wesley was doing and had put a preemptive plan in place. She'd even gotten Aidan to come here and do her dirty work.

But she'd been the one in the bookstore the second time—the one who'd pushed over the shelf. She'd come back, fearing that Maisie knew more than she'd let on. She wanted to eavesdrop—but then she'd nearly been caught.

The money that had been stolen during the robberies had been put in an overseas account. Deana and Perry were planning on retiring and living out their dreams on an island in the Caribbean.

At least they all had answers now.

Tali stepped downstairs and into her bookstore, glad to see the festivities were already in full swing. She'd opened up for the town festival, and Maisie was hard at work behind the coffee counter. Her niece had dressed as Jane Austen for the event.

Meanwhile, Tali had a plastic jack-o'-lantern full

of miniature chocolate bars wrapped in covers to look like classic children's books to hand out to anyone who came by.

It would be a fun night.

She readjusted her trench coat and hat. She'd dressed as her favorite detective.

"Love the costume," Maisie said from across the room. "Sherlock, right?"

"Who else than one of the greatest detectives in literature?"

"Brilliant."

Before Tali could head outside to hand out treats, someone stepped into her shop.

The mayor.

Mac.

Her heart sped.

Then she noticed that he was dressed as . . . Sherlock Holmes also.

Their gazes met, and they burst into laughter.

Mac paused in front of her, still grinning. "Great minds, huh?"

"You can say that again." Tali squeezed his hand. "You look great."

"You too. Although I did consider dressing up as a demented—"

"Dementor," she corrected.

He smiled. "I did consider dressing up as a

Dementor for a moment. Axel says I should read Harry Potter so I can understand the hubbub more."

"There's a reason that series has sold millions of copies and gotten its own theme park." Tali grinned. "I hear you have a costume contest to preside over."

Mac glanced at his watch. "It starts in ten minutes. I wanted to stop by and see you first."

She grinned again. "I'm glad you did."

Their gazes caught.

The amount of gratitude Tali felt for this man continued to grow.

He'd been a real godsend. Despite their history, she thanked God every day for him.

She only regretted that the very thing that bound them was the trouble they'd both encountered.

Mac grabbed her hand and tugged her back into the office area—out of sight from everyone . . . except Sugar, who followed at their feet.

Then Mac stepped closer and pressed his lips against hers.

"You know, the Bible says that in this world we will have troubles," Tali murmured after they pulled apart.

"But we have hope beyond our temporary homes," Mac finished, paraphrasing the rest of the verse. "Our momentary troubles will only work in our favor to make us stronger. Thank goodness for the light at the end of the tunnel."

"Absolutely." Tali grinned.

Mac pushed a blonde hair out of her eyes. "Life has been an adventure these past several months with you in it, Tali."

"Yes, it has been, hasn't it?"

"I can't think of anyone I'd rather experience this adventure with."

Tali reached up and rested her hand against the side of his face. "I couldn't agree more."

They shared one more smile before leaning toward each other and sharing another kiss.

~~~

Thank you so much for reading *Bound by Trouble*. If you enjoyed this book, please consider leaving a review.

COMPLETE BOOK LIST

Squeaky Clean Mysteries:
#1 Hazardous Duty
#2 Suspicious Minds
#2.5 It Came Upon a Midnight Crime (novella)
#3 Organized Grime
#4 Dirty Deeds
#5 The Scum of All Fears
#6 To Love, Honor and Perish
#7 Mucky Streak
#8 Foul Play
#9 Broom & Gloom
#10 Dust and Obey
#11 Thrill Squeaker
#11.5 Swept Away (novella)
#12 Cunning Attractions
#13 Cold Case: Clean Getaway

#14 Cold Case: Clean Sweep

#15 Cold Case: Clean Break

#16 Cleans to an End

While You Were Sweeping, A Riley Thomas Spinoff

The Sierra Files:

#1 Pounced

#2 Hunted

#3 Pranced

#4 Rattled

The Gabby St. Claire Diaries (a Tween Mystery series):

The Curtain Call Caper

The Disappearing Dog Dilemma

The Bungled Bike Burglaries

The Worst Detective Ever

#1 Ready to Fumble

#2 Reign of Error

#3 Safety in Blunders

#4 Join the Flub

#5 Blooper Freak

#6 Flaw Abiding Citizen

#7 Gaffe Out Loud

#8 Joke and Dagger

#9 Wreck the Halls

#10 Glitch and Famous

Raven Remington

Relentless

Holly Anna Paladin Mysteries:

#1 Random Acts of Murder

#2 Random Acts of Deceit

#2.5 Random Acts of Scrooge

#3 Random Acts of Malice

#4 Random Acts of Greed

#5 Random Acts of Fraud

#6 Random Acts of Outrage

#7 Random Acts of Iniquity

Lantern Beach Mysteries

#1 Hidden Currents

#2 Flood Watch

#3 Storm Surge

#4 Dangerous Waters

#5 Perilous Riptide

#6 Deadly Undertow

Lantern Beach Romantic Suspense

Tides of Deception

Shadow of Intrigue

Storm of Doubt

Winds of Danger

Rains of Remorse

Torrents of Fear

Lantern Beach P.D.

On the Lookout

Attempt to Locate

First Degree Murder

Dead on Arrival

Plan of Action

Lantern Beach Escape

Afterglow (a novelette)

Lantern Beach Blackout

Dark Water

Safe Harbor

Ripple Effect

Rising Tide

Lantern Beach Guardians

Hide and Seek

Shock and Awe

Safe and Sound

Lantern Beach Blackout: The New Recruits

Rocco

Axel

Beckett

Gabe

Lantern Beach Mayday

Run Aground

Dead Reckoning

Tipping Point

Lantern Beach Blackout: Danger Rising

Brandon

Dylan

Maddox

Titus

Lantern Beach Christmas

Silent Night

Crime á la Mode

Dead Man's Float

Milkshake Up

Bomb Pop Threat

Banana Split Personalities

Beach Bound Books and Beans Mysteries

Bound by Murder

Bound by Disaster

Bound by Mystery

Bound by Trouble (coming soon)

Vanishing Ranch

Forgotten Secrets

Necessary Risk

Risky Ambition

Deadly Intent

Lethal Betrayal

High Stakes Deception (coming soon)

The Sidekick's Survival Guide

The Art of Eavesdropping

The Perks of Meddling

The Exercise of Interfering

The Practice of Prying

The Skill of Snooping

The Craft of Being Covert

Saltwater Cowboys

Saltwater Cowboy

Breakwater Protector

Cape Corral Keeper

Seagrass Secrets

Driftwood Danger

Unwavering Security

Beach House Mysteries

The Cottage on Ghost Lane

The Inn on Hanging Hill

The House on Dagger Point

School of Hard Rocks Mysteries

The Treble with Murder

Crime Strikes a Chord

Tone Death

Carolina Moon Series

Home Before Dark

Gone By Dark

Wait Until Dark

Light the Dark

Taken By Dark

Suburban Sleuth Mysteries:

Death of the Couch Potato's Wife

Fog Lake Suspense:

Edge of Peril

Margin of Error

Brink of Danger

Line of Duty

Legacy of Lies

Secrets of Shame

Refuge of Redemption

Cape Thomas Series:
Dubiosity
Disillusioned
Distorted

Standalone Romantic Mystery:
The Good Girl

Suspense:
Imperfect
The Wrecking

Sweet Christmas Novella:
Home to Chestnut Grove

Standalone Romantic-Suspense:
Keeping Guard
The Last Target
Race Against Time
Ricochet
Key Witness
Lifeline
High-Stakes Holiday Reunion
Desperate Measures
Hidden Agenda

Mountain Hideaway

Dark Harbor

Shadow of Suspicion

The Baby Assignment

The Cradle Conspiracy

Trained to Defend

Mountain Survival

Dangerous Mountain Rescue

Nonfiction:

Characters in the Kitchen

Changed: True Stories of Finding God through Christian Music (out of print)

The Novel in Me: The Beginner's Guide to Writing and Publishing a Novel (out of print)

ABOUT THE AUTHOR

USA Today has called Christy Barritt's books "scary, funny, passionate, and quirky."

Christy writes both mystery and romantic suspense novels that are clean with underlying messages of faith. Her books have sold more than three million copies and have won the Daphne du Maurier Award for Excellence in Suspense and Mystery, have been twice nominated for the Romantic Times Reviewers' Choice Award, and have finaled for both a Carol Award and Foreword Magazine's Book of the Year.

She is married to her Prince Charming, a man who thinks she's hilarious—but only when she's not trying to be. Christy is a self-proclaimed klutz, an avid music lover who's known for spontaneously bursting into song, and a road trip aficionado.

When she's not working or spending time with her family, she enjoys singing, playing the guitar, and exploring small, unsuspecting towns where people have no idea how accident-prone she is.

Find Christy online at:
www.christybarritt.com
www.facebook.com/christybarritt
www.twitter.com/cbarritt

Sign up for Christy's newsletter to get information on all of her latest releases here: **www.christybarritt. com/newsletter-sign-up/**

www.ingramcontent.com/pod-product-compliance
Lightning Source LLC
Chambersburg PA
CBHW021153260326
41798CB00029B/374